THE SEA

THE SEA

SWATI GUHA

Translated from the Bengali by
V. RAMASWAMY

An Imprint of Antonym Collections
USA | INDIA

Published by Antonym Collections
151, D.H Road, Kolkata - 700104, India
theantonymmag.com

ISBN 978-81-971522-7-6

Cover design & Typeset by Mom Chatterjee

To

Ms. Anita Agnihotri

Who I found as a shade on a terribly sunny day

Chapter 1

'What do you do on the days when you don't have college, I mean on holidays?'

'Nothing really.'

'I didn't get you. What do you do? After all, the days of college race by.'

'No, it's not exactly like that.'

'Then how is it? That's what I'd like to know. Of course, if you have any objection to telling me, then let it be; you don't have to tell me.'

'No, no, it's nothing like that. Actually…'

'Actually, you don't even like to talk to me.'

'Arey, no, no…'

'Actually, you don't even like to talk…'

'Perhaps that's partly true.'

'Why partly? It's entirely true.'

'No, it's not entirely true. Actually… actually, I've lost the habit of talking to anyone but myself.'

'I know.'

'You don't know anything.'

'I love this notion of yours that I don't know anything. And so, I get some more time to get to know you.'

'Who on earth am I? And I don't understand why you want to know me.'

'If nothing else, I've at least been your flatmate for the last one and a half years. You surely agree about that? Or is it that you don't even see me as an equal?'

'Of course not; why would that be? Actually, in the last one and a half years, you have been in this flat for no more than a month and a half, all told. And to tell the truth, your work, your movements, your way of life, and so on—at least so far as I could make out—are all so alien to me, or I should say, to my imagination, that I had no interest in any of that.'

'Let it be, I'm most fortunate today.'

'Why's that?'

'Well, right in the morning I could get you to agree to sit and have tea with me!'

'Look, whatever you might think of me, I'm going to sleep all day today. If I feel like it, I'll get up in the evening and cook, or else I'll eat instant noodles.'

'So, tell me, Tinni, do you like being alone all the time?'

'Alone? How am I alone? I'm together with quite a few "I"s all the time. The friendships, love affairs, and quarrels go on between them all the time. I get tired resolving those. So how am I alone? By the way, how did you get to know this name of mine? Nobody in Bombay knows it. And all those who used to call me by that name have forgotten about me entirely.'

'You see, I do know. Actually, I try to know. That's what's called "homework."'

'Don't do that.'

'Why?'

'If all the nice things that Rohini's said about me are displaced, it would be my loss.'

'How so?'

'It's because you pay half the rent that I can still dream of staying in this flat in Bombay.'

'Why a dream? You really live here. And most of the time you're alone here.'

'Actually, even now, as soon as I wake up, my eyes first see the blue of the sea. But that would not have been possible without Rohini. A balcony on the eighteenth floor that leans over the sea, in Tardeo, a place like this—after all, it's a dream. Instead, if I somehow managed to get a job, I might have stayed as a paying guest in Nala Sopara or Shanpara. Maybe not even that. Who knows…'

'There's nothing to be so dejected about.'

'I can't really say there's nothing…'

'Why?'

'How about all that being the topic for this evening?'

'Why?'

'Didn't I tell you I've planned to sleep all day today?'

'I know you're always eager to avoid me.'

'Why would that be? You're so famous! Even you don't know the number of fans you have. And I'm merely a teacher!'

'My fame and all that…is that why you avoid me?'

'Why should I avoid you? Whenever there's something, if you're here, I tell you, or otherwise, I speak to you over the phone.'

'Yes, you do, but that's about the rent, bills, tax and all that!'

'No, I also try to remember and tell you the various messages that your friends come and leave for you.'

'That's why I'm grateful to you.'

'I don't think about all that. You, too, are inconvenienced

because of me at times. I don't like that.'

'Why would I be inconvenienced because of you? After all, it was written in our terms of reference that we can spend time in our own rooms, as we wish. And that we won't use the common space in such a way that the other resident is inconvenienced.'

'I know that you try to be careful so that I am not inconvenienced.'

'Me and careful? The two can never go together!'

'Who knows, I'm not so aware.'

'You're aware, alright. As soon as you feel that you're becoming a bit more flexible, you start building the wall. Please, Tinni, why don't you keep your professorial stance away for today! Please!'

'Don't you have a shoot today?'

'No.'

'Don't you have anything? Friends, etcetera?'

'No, but why are you getting so irritated? You don't even want me to be at home!'

'Arey, not at all. Didn't I say I feel like sleeping today!'

'Alright. I'll cook your favorite meal today. Tell me, what would you like to eat?'

'Don't invite calamity by asking me that.'

'Why, when you cooked for me that day, was it calamitous for you?'

'It's not that. Actually, if I want to have *shukto* or *posto* now, then obviously that would be calamitous for you!'

'Listen, I've learned East Bengali cuisine by heart. But I think *posto* is a delicacy of West Bengal!'

'Ore Baba! Are you planning to quit modeling and enter the restaurant business?'

'Wow! A wonderful idea! Do you have any idea how many millions are needed to start a restaurant in Bombay?'

'No, not at all. I break out in perspiration when I hear talk of lakhs-thousands. And if it's in millions, I might even get a heart attack.

'I find this talk of yours very strange!'

'Why's that? I really can't think clearly about big figures, or about earning or spending a lot of money. Actually, there's no chance of the college salary rising and reaching a hundred thousand; that's why I'm still used to thinking in thousands.'

'I know you don't think of me as anything but a racing rat.'

'Believe me, I don't think about all that. Actually, I don't think about anything. Especially something that's not directly connected to me. I'd like to simply remove myself from the situation around me and survive. Perhaps it's because of the fear of this selfishness of mine being discovered that I've become used to concealing myself.'

'And do you think I flaunt myself too much?'

'No. I really don't think about anything like that.'

'I've brought something for you. Promise me you'll accept it!'

'What is it?'

'Something.'

'My mind does not consent to giving my word without knowing what it is.'

'Tell your mind that it's a picture. Whose, what—don't ask me all that.'

'But why would you give it to me?'

'Just like that! You're so wary about everything!'

'You're right, I am wary! Actually, you know, I always thought there had to be some meaning to whatever I did. Maybe that's why I still feel a bit afraid, even now! The search for meaning has tossed me around so much; that's why I'm afraid.'

'Would you like another cup of tea?'

'No. You have it. I'm going to sleep today.'

'Today, after a long time, I really feel like staying at home. If the sleeping is in order to avoid me, then please go to your own room right now. And if you're really feeling sleepy, then don't go.'

'Perhaps you're an expert in creating such upside-down reasoning!'

'My expertise? You can find out about that from fashion magazines and film world gossip! But you surely don't read all that!'

'Do you know everything about what I read or don't read?'

'No, I don't know everything. But I guess some of it.'

'How do you do that?'

'You teach literature. You're always in the company of books.'

'God! The things you say…'

'But I've seen you reading a book in the kitchen too, on the dining table, on the balcony…'

'Ore Baba! Do you have divine sight? You know so much about my movements even without being in Bombay.'

'Didn't I tell you, it's the network!'

'Tell me, you haven't placed cameras and so on in the common areas, have you?'

'Do you have any particular reason to think I'm so mean?'

'Arey Baba, I didn't say that. You speak so confidently about my various habits that it makes me feel uneasy.'

'Think about it, you too know about some similar habits of mine.'

'Who knows! Maybe because I never really thought specifically about that, I'm not confident.'

'There's no need to be confident about me.'

'When did I say that was very necessary for me!'

'Arey no. Don't take it otherwise! Please!'

'I'm not at all interested in your habits!'

'Please, Tinni, I won't say such stupid things again. What I really wanted to say was that you, too, know about some of my habits. For instance, I play the music system very loud, I keep having tea or coffee, and I smoke while working, even in the kitchen. Do you remember, in the beginning, when we would meet in the kitchen about once every two months, and how annoyed you'd be when you saw me?'

'Why would I be annoyed? I used to feel uncomfortable when I suddenly entered the kitchen to find you there with a glass of alcohol in your hand and a cigarette dangling from your lips, carrying out culinary revolutions. And then your clothes.'

'Sorry, I sometimes forget that I am sharing the apartment with a woman. Tell me, Tinni, what would you like to eat this morning?'

'What would *you* like to eat?'

'Why? Will you make it?'

'No way.'

'Alright then. I'll make it. Tell me what you'd like to eat. Would you like a French omelet? I do that very well!

'You're really into all things French, aren't you?'

'You could say that. French cuisine, films, music, paintings, and especially, French women. I like them a lot.'

'Is your girlfriend French?'

'My first girlfriend was Sumedha. She was a Konkani Brahmin. Her folks came to know about us just before the Class 12 exams. And that was the end. Sumedha! Oh, how exceptionally beautiful she was! She lives in Bahrain now, with her doctor husband and their two daughters.'

'Are you still in touch with her?'

'Can't really say that. But last year, at a show in Sharjah, a lady suddenly came to the make-up room to meet me, saying she was a relative.'

'That's like something out of a film!'

'You could say that.'

'And what happened then?'

'What could happen? She said her daughters wanted my

autograph. I promised to have dinner with them the next day. But I didn't go, you know. I don't know whether I should have done that, but I just didn't have the slightest desire to sit and have idiotic conversations with that fat woman and her husband. Nor did I want to be called "Uncle" and be talked to so-sweetly by her daughters.'

'You could have phoned and informed her.'

'I didn't do that myself; the tour manager did it.'

'Let me have a shower. I'll honour your invitation after that.'

'Can't you shower a bit later today?'

'Actually, I'm just not used to having anything except a cup of tea before I shower.'

'Can't you try to escape that habit for one day? You'll see what fun it can be! Tell me, have you ever spent the whole day in unstoppable conversation?'

'Yes, but I don't want to remember all that anymore.'

'Why's that?'

'Who likes to scrape the heart and awaken pain?'

'If not anyone else, I do know that you love that very much.'

'You know nothing!'

'But let me make the omelet! Would you like to learn?'

'No. I don't feel like doing anything today. Believe me, I really wanted to sleep.'

'Good. The wish is apparently now in the past tense. That's fine for me.'

'I had to write all night. I went to sleep only at 5 o'clock. But I couldn't sleep. I got up and saw that you were sleeping in the drawing room. I thought you'd be disturbed if there was any sound in the kitchen, and so I went back to bed.'

'You could have made me a cup of tea and called me!'

'I never think of such things. You know that very well.'

'I've never met anyone as peaceful and indifferent as you. Believe me, that's why I'm curious about you.'

'That I'm peaceful or indifferent—all that's make-believe. It's a veil I carry. Perhaps it's part of a concerted attempt to tame the impossible inner storms.'

'You have an amazing relationship with the sea, isn't it?'

'That may be. I don't really know.'

'Why don't you sit here? I can't see your face. We can talk while I'm making my special omelet.'

'I've been jabbering away since morning.'

'It's me who's jabbering away. You're just going through the motions, disinterestedly.'

'Interest… disinterest… you discern so much. You'd have become famous even if you had been a psychiatrist instead of an actor.'

'Is your writing also as somber as you?'

'Who told you about my writing?'

'Why do you always think of me as an illiterate and an ignoramus?'

'Why should that be? I know you studied engineering.'

'Wow! How did you know that?'

'Arey, before leaving, Rohini tutored me for two months. Night and day. She imparted all the possible training so that I could live by myself in Bombay. There was no end to her concern for me. She was the one who was most concerned about the flat. She knew that if I stayed here, I would be well. And so, she thought of letting it out as a shared flat.'

'When you heard about me, you objected a lot, didn't you?'

'I don't know if I objected very much, but yes, I did object a little. But after all, you were the brother of Rohini's childhood friend, Shreya, and so I wasn't worried. It took me a little while to take in everything.'

'You still haven't been able to take everything in, Tinni, or else you wouldn't have avoided me so much.'

'Where do I avoid you? I'm not much of a social person. That's why I don't go out of my way to talk or get acquainted unless it's necessary.'

'Let's set aside any other necessity, but don't you need to talk to people?'

'Didn't I tell you that I've fashioned a kind of means whereby I keep talking to myself, and so there's no time for anything else?'

'Don't you think your stock of words is diminishing? That your vocal cords are becoming defunct because of non-use?'

'Why would that be? I wouldn't be able to retain my job if I only spoke to myself inwardly in college. And I have to talk so much and in so many classes that it's better to allow the vocal cords some rest for the remaining time.'

'But in class, you only engage in the same old kind of talk— the course and dictating notes!'

'I can't dictate memorized notes. I lack that skill. I try to teach in a fresh way each day. That's why every year, and for that matter, even in two consecutive classes, I can't talk using the same diction. The way of teaching also varies according to how prepared the students are.'

'I wish I were your student!'

'Oh, I haven't told you, but a colleague of mine somehow discovered that you live in this apartment. And so, a barrage of questions come to me.'

'And how do you respond?'

'I don't respond at all!'

'That's good.'

'Yes, I know that.'

'What do you know?'

'There are no onions in a French omelet.'

'Wow! You know that too!'

'I don't know as much as you. I know just a little bit.'

'Were you singing late at night yesterday?'

'How did you know?'

'I didn't know. I heard.'

'The party was going on in your part all evening. When I returned from my walk, I saw that a friend of yours was busy cooking in the kitchen.'

'I'm sorry. It's a big bother for you on such days. Actually, Minal had returned from Canada after a long time. And I managed to get two more people.'

'Did they leave last night itself?'

'At night, meaning it was four thirty when they left. But I'm going to be terribly busy for the next month. I have to travel around the world, more or less. The gaps in the schedule are also very limited this time. That's why I was reluctant to take it up.'

'So, you're going to be away from Bombay for a long time now?'

'You're glad to hear that, aren't you?'

'Oh God! Did I say that? You visit so many countries!'

'You too could travel during the college vacations.'

'You don't have the slightest clue about the lives of people like me! That's why it's possible for you to think like that.'

'Why? Why do you say that?'

'Do you know how much it costs to go abroad?'

'I know.'

'Like hell you do! If you did, you wouldn't suggest traveling abroad during the holidays to any person teaching in a college.'

'Look here; you're not exactly as poor as you try to project yourself to be!'

'When did I ever project myself as being poor? Do people become poor if they can't go abroad? Actually, I think people in your profession don't have the slightest notion about who the poor in our country are!'

'Please don't rebuke me. I know far less than you. I don't regret that at all. Nor am I proud of it. But it would be nice if you were a little more normal!'

'That means you think I am abnormal!'

'It's not fair. I say one thing, and you draw out another interpretation!'

'You know very well that I don't have the slightest desire or time to draw out anything whatsoever. Anyway, you didn't offend me!'

'And this great indifference with which you avoid me, do you think that's nice?'

'Why would you feel bad about it, tell me? Your fame, your friends, you have lots and lots of all that… I can't think of any reason why a quiet and insignificant person like me should matter at all to you.'

'By the way, Tinni, I have heard from Rohini that right from your childhood, you were top of the class in everything.'

'Oh God, Rohini could never have said that. In everything, I mean, after all, I never did anything much.'

'Rohini said your academic background was fantastic. She said you sing beautifully. That no one could equal you in debating. And that you write very well.'

'Is that all Rohini said?

'I know that even a single thing isn't made up.'

'Do you know what's the masculine gender of PRAJNAPARAMITA?'

'Why?'

'I'm wondering how it would be if your name was changed to that. But, of course, it's difficult to carry out such experiments on famous people like you! By the way, who taught you to cook?'

'My mother, a little bit, and mostly by myself.'

'But Bengali mothers never encourage their sons as far as learning cooking goes.'

'Did you learn from your mother?'

'No, in this respect, I'm entirely self-educated! Although my mother was an exceptional cook.'

'Why? Does she not cook now?'

'Maybe she does. Maybe she doesn't. I don't know.'

'Why?'

'Your homework is incomplete. Forget about those things. How's the omelet doing?'

'Here, I'm tossing the tomatoes; two more minutes. Are you terribly hungry?'

'Not at all. I'm not in the habit of eating very much in the morning.'

'How did you become such a vegetarian despite being Bengali?'

'Who told you I'm a vegetarian!'

'I've observed you cooking from time to time. And so I asked. By the way, Tinni, I want to apologize to you for something. Promise me, you won't let me down!'

'First of all, why should you apologize to me? And why on earth would I let you down? To begin the day with all this, I don't like it at all. And please don't call me Tinni. Rohini too never called me Tinni.'

'I'm sorry! If you don't like to be called Tinni, I won't do that. And maybe you know that I also call Rohini by her pet name. And I never referred to any of Shreya's friends as "Didi" and so on!'

'That's your business; I have nothing to say about that.'

'That's all right. But please tell me what name I should call you by.'

'You just love to talk, don't you?'

'No. Not with everyone. It's not part of my profession to talk very much. Everyone regards everyone else as a competitor and avoids them. No one talks much except for outright fabrication. That's why, whenever there's some talk within one's own circle, it becomes the subject of gossip. That's the reason I'm tired of all the measured behavior. It makes me angry. But that can damage one's career. And so, one has to do yoga, meditation, and all that!'

'All right. You can call me…'

'Can I call you "Sea"?'

'No, no… Not at all…!'

'In that case, until an acceptable name is decided upon, I'll continue calling you Tinni. Please don't prohibit that.'

'What does it matter whether I prohibit or not?'

'To get back to what I was saying, Leena annoyed you very much that day. Despite my telling her repeatedly not to, she just didn't heed me. Please forgive me for that.'

'What's there to apologize so profusely about? She needed to use the internet, and so she came to my room and did that with my permission. I can't see anything objectionable in that.'

'Alright, Tinni, do you think you're great in all respects?'

'Not at all! I've never ever had occasion to think of myself as great in any respect. And as far as Leena is concerned, I hardly know her. I've seen her coming to visit you from time to time, and that too only if I encounter her on my way in or out.'

'Didn't it occur to you even once that Leena went to your room simply to annoy you?'

'Not at all! Why on earth would she suddenly think of annoying me?'

'Tinni, I have to know you. Believe me, I won't be at peace unless I know you a bit. Leena went to you purely and simply to annoy you. She kept on asking me about you. I could not give her satisfying answers. That's why she decided to go and spend some time with you so that she could find out about you.'

'So, what did she find out? Did she tell you?'

'She only told me that you were from another planet!'

'Is that why you've held me up with breakfast this morning to ask about that planet?'

'It's not that. But I really want to know you. Since a long time. I've tried to convince myself that you're not like me or that I'm not like you. But still, I don't know why your presence keeps getting entangled with all my thoughts.'

'Don't do that at all. I'm so tied up with myself that I'm unwilling to grant anything to anyone other than myself. Mornings-afternoons-nights are full of my soliloquy. Except when I'm teaching, it's extremely difficult for me to relate to anyone on any matter.'

'That's why one is so eager to know you even a little bit— believe me, just a tiny bit. How is this person able to keep herself so far away from everything?'

'Where am I able to keep myself afar?'

'Why? You spend the whole day, from morning to night, without seeing another person's face or speaking to another person.'

'I don't know what there is to be so surprised about. But suddenly, after so long, why are you concerned about my routine? I never think about what you're doing, or why you do whatever you're doing. Such things just never enter my thoughts.'

'That's why I'm amazed at you! Believe me, I really want to; I find pretexts to be able to spend a little bit of time with you.'

'Don't say such things. It makes me uncomfortable.'

'You know, Tinni, I've secretly listened to you sing many times.'

'No. I don't know.'

'Don't you want to know? You could at least be angry with me, Tinni.'

'I did get angry a couple of times so far. But I didn't want you to know. Of course, on one occasion, I specifically wanted you to know!'

'When was that, Tinni? Was it about taking down a container from the kitchen shelf?'

'Let it be; you recalled it at once. That means you shouldn't have any doubts about my capacity to get angry!'

'Not just when you got angry, I remember many more things too.'

'Many more things like?'

'Your impossibly sexy back! The amazing fit of your black blouse! The awesome way in which you tuck the sari anchal at the waist. Everything. I remember everything, Tinni!'

'Will the omelet get done today? Or would it be tastier to take it out of the fridge and eat it cold later?'

'Will you sing a song for me today, Tinni?'

'I can offer you a cup of coffee in exchange for the omelet. Filter coffee. Would you like that? Ground and filtered by me.'

'Are you offering that in place of the song?'

'I'm not offering it in exchange for anything. If you want it, let me know. I'll have the omelet and go for my shower.'

'I'll cook for you today. Can you tell me what exactly you'd like to eat?'

'*Alu posto* and *alu bhaja*.'

'Just that?'

'No, with rice.'

'I want to get your permission for something today.'

'Don't be so formal. I get terribly scared!'

'Why? Am I becoming more and more scary?'

'I don't know! Perhaps it's about myself that I'm most scared.'

'I love to hear such talk every now and then!'

'What kind of talk?'

'This business of being scared of me. All that.'

'It's not you. I told you the fear is about myself.'

'I'd like to see that one flash of Tinni's true self! That single flash would be like a bolt of lightning for me!'

'To a person like you, whose trajectory in life is only towards advancement, someone like me is nothing but a museum piece!'

'You know everything, don't you!'

'No, I don't. I don't know anything. I don't have an interest in knowing either.'

'In that case, just finish eating quietly.'

'Alright, I'll keep quiet. We'll talk again tomorrow.'

'Please don't punish me!'

'Where am I punishing you?'

Chapter 2

'I was able to create a bit of an opportunity today to talk to you. It's hard work! So please don't vow to be silent. Anyway... I say, will you permit me to enter your room once today? I've wanted to suddenly enter so many times! But you're so distant that I couldn't gather the courage to do that. You're only in the adjacent room. If I want, I can synchronize even my breathing with yours! Yet, I haven't had the chance to see your room even once.'

'Such things never occurred to me!'

'You don't have the slightest interest whatsoever in me! Speaking to me over the phone or... let it be. Tinni, I believe your room is extremely beautiful; ever since Leena told me that, I've been dying to see it.'

'God! You seem to have been entirely taken in by what Leena said!'

'Look here, Leena has nothing positive to say in her life about anyone except herself. That's Leena. But after talking to you for about an hour, she was what's called entranced! How you talk, your

room, the books and so on, the music, the collection of paintings—
you could say she's just fascinated by everything.'

'Leena called me and said she wanted to wear my kind of bindis.
She asked where she could buy them. I told her I'd get it for her.'

'She said she's going to take a crash course from you on how
to wear a sari before her next film.'

'She called me last night.'

'What did she say?'

'I suppose all your friends are as crazy as you!'

'Why? Why do you say that?'

'She asked me to be her costume designer for her forthcoming
film.'

'What's crazy about that?'

'I'm just a student of literature from a small town. My profession
is teaching. The tastes, preferences, and so on of the world of cinema
are a million miles away.'

'But Leena told me she was serious about this. She's going to
speak to the director too. She wants to get all her costumes done
by you.'

'I'll go crazy now. Please! Please! Don't tell me all this. I need
my solitude. If I don't have that I won't survive.'

'What's that solitude? Can I know something about that?'

'Please tell Leena that I'm not into all that.'

'Leena said that she's apparently never met anyone with as
keen a dressing sense as yours.'

'Just how much of me has she seen?'

'However much she's seen! Anyway, tell Leena whatever you
have to. I've got nothing to do with that…'

'You can't just say that you have nothing to do with that. Leena
is your friend. She took your permission before coming to my room.'

'No, that's not correct! She didn't come with my permission.
I told her repeatedly not to bother you. She didn't listen. Her

curiosity about you knew no bounds.'

'All that's your business! I have nothing to say.'

'But you didn't tell me whether or not I'm allowed to see your room!'

'We're talking here; we're chatting here. We quarreled a bit too!'

'Meaning you're not going to allow me to enter your room. But I didn't have any such issues when you went into my room.'

'I never wanted to go to your room. Not even when the painting was happening. But the painters were just not willing to enter the room of someone as famous as you all by themselves. I requested them several times. Finally, since they were adamant about it, I had to go to the room.'

'And what did you see there?'

'There wasn't much scope for me to be fascinated by what I saw.'

'That's why I ask—will it be very painful for you if you give me a chance?

'A lot of things have run out in the kitchen. I have to stop by the market while returning tomorrow.'

'Would you like to go this evening?'

'Where?'

'To the market.'

'No.'

'Why? Are you afraid of being disgraced by stepping out with me?'

'I grew up in such a small town that even if the shadows of a boy and girl came together on the street, there would be a discussion about it even in the collectorate. And so, I've had to hear so much about being disgraced! Let it be, I've got so used to doing my chores by myself that I don't feel like attaching anyone else to that.'

'You've not had these habits eternally. You formed them. And so, if you begin doing something else, that too will soon become a habit.'

'I don't want to form any new habits. I don't have the courage. You know age brings another kind of wisdom. Experience advises me to stay alone.'

'Experience teaches me too—never stop! Walk, run, sprint! And sometimes it tells me to sit for a while. Believe me, returning at dawn after a night shoot, I've gone up to your door so many times and then turned back. I just wanted to see you once. And standing in front of your shut door, I got an amazing fragrance. But that fragrance never invited me to come near. It wafted in from the sea and then became one with the sea again.'

'You're an outright…'

'Go and have your shower. I'll wait here. The picture I've brought for you—I wanted to go to your room to see where exactly in your room it would look best, or at least where I'd like it. But since you're not agreeable, I won't insist. I'll go when you allow me to.'

'Don't say that; it makes me feel guilty.'

'It's me who's guilty! I'm the one who thinks Tinni is close to me. But for Tinni, I'm far away. And between me and Tinni stand our professions and the apparent difference between our lives!'

'Why do you say *apparent*? It is a fact that our socio-economic status is so different that we can never think alike. And I have no discomfort whatsoever about that because I know that, and I heed it too. My requirements are so removed from all that and are so real that I don't even get the chance to think about anything else. And one could say that I have been able to. I'm free from any attachments with anyone in regard to my tastes, preferences, likes and dislikes, and I've been able to survive by avoiding conflict.'

'Tinni, do you know my nickname?'

'Yes.'

'I never heard you calling me by that even once.'

'Because there was no need to.'

'Say you don't want to either!'

'Yes, you could say that!'

'One can't discern any outward problem in you. And yet you readily behave like a plastic doll.'

'Who knows. I can't tell you. Why bother! Let me go for my shower first. You take it easy too. You've been at work for me since morning!'

'Would you like to eat pomfret? I have some in the fridge. *Patrani Macchi?* My mother's recipe. It's been a long time since I made it. Let me try today. Go for your shower. But come back and sit here!'

'Alright.'

'Listen, will you do me a favor? Just for today, finish your shower quickly. I'll be terribly bored otherwise.'

'There have been many days when we have both been at home, and let alone talking, we haven't even seen each other! You didn't even know whether I was home or not, and I…'

'You don't have to go over that again.'

'Why?'

'Because my being home, most of the time, is so noisy that it's impossible for you to be unaware.'

'Nevertheless, it's not that I had a problem with all that all the time. You know, actually, when no one's there, solitude too becomes insipid. That's why, when you or others make a commotion , my own *tapasya* becomes even more interesting.'

'The whole day with you today. The whole day with Tinni. And so, the less you are available the greater my loss! Hurry up and finish your shower. I'm waiting.'

'Is having me there all there is? I remembered something I'd written.'

'Do tell me…'

'Tell you what?'

'What you wrote.'

'*Shamne eshe jetuku dao / shey shob kichu tomar / araal theke ja kichhu pai / shey shob shudhu amar.*'

'That which you give directly to me / Those are yours / That which I get out of you / Is entirely mine.'

'Yes, it could more or less be put that way.'

'Why, wasn't it correct? Oh, I didn't get it, right?'

'Rohini never told me you read poetry. But she did tell me that you were a very good student, excellent in sports, had an exceptional sense of humor, and so on, and sang a thousand praises!'

'I owe Rohini a lot. If she hadn't left Bombay at that time, I wouldn't have come to this flat. I wouldn't have known that there is a person called Tinni on this planet.'

'There's a ghost called Tinni! Stay away from her!'

'Tinni is possessed by a ghost. I wish I could take her away from it—there, far away. If only one could take Tinni across the sea to the other shore, that would be fantastic!'

'Tinni died, and Achira has been trying without letup to stay around.'

'Tell me, Achira means lightning, doesn't it?'

'Yes! You know so much!'

'You're making fun of me; go ahead. Every now and then, I feel like calling you *Spark*! Sometimes *Neel*—from the blue sea!'

'You have to improvise the dialogue quite often in your films, isn't it?'

'Why did you suddenly think of that?'

'You see, when one talks to any woman, exactly when, what tone, diction, and vocabulary should be used so that it stands out a bit and is of a different kind—all that is also a matter of your acting prowess.'

'At last, whatever the subject might be, it's indeed a milestone for me that Tinni views what I said as being somewhat different.'

'And that's the last milestone on the map of the earth. After that lies the great void.'

'I know that. Once one gets there, there's no question of returning!'

'I have no wish to win any war of words with you at this moment. We can continue after my shower.'

'I'll marinate the pomfret in the meantime. So, hurry up. Today's colour is blue.'

'What do you mean?'

'Figure it out. I know that you're adept at reading between the lines.'

'You are the Ultimate Lord, Brahma! There's nothing you don't know!'

'I may not be Brahma, but yes, I guess I am a Lord given that my name is "Dev." May I smoke a cigarette on your balcony?'

'Why? Is smoking prohibited on your balcony?'

'It's not that; I asked just like that. Besides, I've seen you sitting by yourself and smoking there.'

'Are you a spy?'

'For whom?'

'How would I know that? Why do you secretly look at where I read books, smoke, or dry my hair?'

'It's because you object to me looking at you directly, so I have to do it secretly.'

'Why do you need to see? I never feel like doing something like that.'

'There are so many things that you don't like to do. It may well be that I don't dislike some of those things.'

'There's no shortage of people in this world who want you. Touchwood—you have a large number of friends and fans. So why do you object so much if only I—someone who's extremely ordinary, introverted, and solitary—stay away from all that and be as I am?'

'I have no objection to that. I only want a bit of friendship from you.'

'All my desire and eagerness to make friends have gone. I want to settle into myself. Don't force me; being alone is kind of meditative for me. Of course, that's not just about being physically alone; even in my mind, there's an image built up about myself, and I want to live up to that.'

'Do you know what exactly that is?'

'I think I do.'

'What's it like? What's your philosophy, in short?'

'I'll study and teach because I need a job to survive, and I like to teach. I'll write the way I want. If the opportunity arises, I'll get it published, or else not. I'll sing because I like to do that. Not because someone will appreciate it, or someone likes it. What clothes or makeup I wear—everything will be according to my likes and will embody my choice. I'll talk the way I like. That's why a large window and a balcony are essential for me. The sea is a gift from Rohini. Rohini is like a goddess in my eyes. She has been like a shade in my life, which I needed badly on a terribly sunny day. You too helped me in that regard by sharing the flat's rent at the right time, and are still doing so. And so, I'm grateful to you too.'

'My being here is just a coincidence. It need not have been Dev; it could have been anyone.'

'Maybe so, but even now, sometimes I wonder what I'd do if Rohini ever thinks of selling the flat. I don't think she has any plans to come back here.'

'Yes, she once told me too that if we don't want to continue paying the bank's monthly instalments, she'll then think of selling the flat. She wanted to know if I was interested. But everything depends on you. Rohini will not do anything contrary to your liking.'

'I know that. A lot of her decisions involve me. Sometimes

I think I should make some other arrangement. But if I did that unilaterally, that would amount to insulting Rohini. I can't do that. It was just when I sank into solitude that Rohini gave me a place to keep my feelings alive. Or else, Achira too would have died and turned into a ghost long ago.'

'Did you know someone called Rudra when you used to teach in the university?'

'Rudra? In which department?'

'Economics.'

'Rudra in Economics? I can't recall anyone. What's his surname?'

'Ray. His father was the dean.'

'Dr. Arijit Ray? But his son is Shounak Ray.'

'Yes, Shounak's pet name is Rudra.'

'I didn't know that. Was he the basis of your homework?'

'A bit of it, you could say, but not the whole thing.'

'How do you know Shounak?'

'Rudra and I were together in school from Class 1 to Class 12.'

'Okay! They're from Chandigarh. I've heard that Shounak was a brilliant student.'

'He was. I wasn't exactly Mister Failure either! Rudra's Ma and my Ma both studied in the same college and teach in the same college now.'

'Tell me something: has your Ma ever come here to your flat?'

'You'd have seen her if she had.'

'There's no reason for you to think that I know everything about who visits you, and when they visit you.'

'It's not that. If my Ma had come here, she would have met you. After all, you too teach in a college. And live by yourself. An emancipated woman. Ma likes all that a lot.'

'It's good to know that you still keep track of your parents' likes and dislikes.'

'That's why I told you. Try to talk with me a bit; you'll like it. I'm not a bad sort.'

'I know that.'

'How's that?'

'If you were a bad sort, Rohini would not have allowed you to live in her flat. It's because she believed that I would not be inconvenienced that she requested you to stay here.'

'Don't say 'request', say she gave me the opportunity. I was seriously thinking about leaving the paying guest accommodation I was in. And I wasn't in a position to buy something of my own either. It's inconvenient for my work if the location isn't right. So, all things considered, Rohini's proposal was like winning a lottery. I did think about the fact that you were in a completely different profession, and so on. Although from my childhood I have been seeing two completely different kinds of people living together beautifully.'

'Your Baba is a businessman, isn't he?'

'Yes. My Baba has a lot of money. You could say his social status is also quite elevate. But Ma still teaches in college. In my childhood, I sometimes saw problems arise because of that. But as I grew older, the problems related to me. Ma wanted me to continue my studies for as long as I wanted. Baba wanted me to go to business school. He wanted me to get a foreign degree—expand his business and all that.'

'And yet you suddenly became a model and a model-turned-actor...'

'You could say it happened suddenly. It started when I went to Delhi to study engineering. I got quite a bit of money for a small assignment on the college ramp. My picture was published in *India Today*. A senior in college had just set up an advertising agency then. He was searching for a new face. He wanted someone who would work for less pay. He gave me a break. That's it, it kept moving after that. I got my degree and won the Gladrags contest. And I finally moved to Bombay.'

'That's where the first difference between you and me lies.'

'What's that?'

'Your winning and coming here, while mine is a tale of defeats.'

'It's a defeat only if you think about it that way, but if you view your defeat as something that actually shows the way to victory, then it won't seem so bad.'

'All that does not trouble me any more. Now perhaps I could say that the bad feeling has decreased a lot. As long as Rohini was here, she didn't want me to think that I ever had a past.'

'That's why, after Rohini left, you always think you're alone, and gaze at the sea and set your words afloat.'

'Nothing can be set afloat on the sea. Whatever I put out comes back to me again. That's how our exchanges take place.'

'Can't you give something if someone doesn't return it?'

'I wouldn't even know whether something was given unless it was returned.'

'Whatever you give will come back, but in a completely new form. How would that be?'

'I'm past thinking about all that. Do you know that I calculate how much money there will be altogether, between my provident fund, gratuity, and savings account, so that I can retire, go to Pondicherry, and await death?'

'Tell me, Tinni, how do you go to college?'

'Why do you ask?'

'Just like that. I want to know.'

'I go by taxi most days. Sometimes, I take a bus. I have to take a taxi while going from here most of the time. Sometimes, while returning, I might walk back if I feel like it.'

'Do you like walking?'

'Very much. I love Bombay because there are so many places in this city where one can walk peacefully along the sea.'

'I've seen you walking by the Nehru Centre many times on your way back home.'

'When Rohini was here, we often parked the car at Chowpatty, walked the entire stretch of Marine Drive, and then returned home.'

'Can I tell you something, Tinni?'

'You said so many things just like that; why do you suddenly ask for my permission?'

'Because I'm scared of whether you'll stop talking to me once I say it.'

'Then don't say something like that.'

'All calculations are straightforward and simple for you, aren't they?'

'Not at all. I've seen so many bends in life that I'm scared now. Lanes, by-lanes… I don't like them anymore. Just walk on the broad street. And fall asleep when you get tired. That's best.'

'Tinni, ever since you arranged my room so beautifully after the flat was painted, I find it very difficult to mess it all up. But sometimes, when I'm in a hurry, I can't find certain things. I then think I should call you and ask whether you know where it might be.'

'I don't know about everything. The painter was a young chap, Raju; he's a fan of yours. He had put back every piece of paper carefully. While he was rearranging the room, he was asking me from time to time whether something should be kept in a particular place or somewhere else. By the way, now that you've mentioned it, I moved around the furniture and changed the seating arrangement without asking you. I moved around the pictures as well. I asked Raju to move the music system, television, and so on. Raju was asking me about you.'

'Like what?'

'What you eat, how long you work out for, what you do when you're at home, all that.'

'What did you tell him?'

'I told him that I wouldn't really be able to tell him everything. He took my phone number. He'll phone me to find out whether you're here or not. And then he'll come to meet you at your convenience. He wants to know whether you're satisfied with the painting done by them. He asked me over the phone what you thought about it.'

'What did you tell him?'

'You used a particular word and that's what I told him.'

'Oh, you could have given a good report.'

'I told him you said "excellent."'

'Not that. He's a young chap. Perhaps he would have liked it more if you elaborated a bit more.'

'If you had elaborated that to me, I would surely have told him. I wouldn't have been stingy.'

'So, you managed to chide me on this pretext!'

'Did I chide you? When was that?'

'That I did not elaborate and should have. I accept. But do you know why I didn't? Since I'm scared of you, I keep everything I say low-key. I think it would amount to bothering you otherwise. Raju's work is incomparable. But really, you were the mastermind behind that. If I bring that up, there'll be no end to your discomfort. That's why I always try to conceal myself from you. I know that if I end up ruining your peace, I'll never be able to forgive myself for that.'

'Ore Baba, I never thought about all that! Ever. Listen, let me give you Raju's number. Give him a call. He'll be over the moon.'

'I don't know about the moon. Give me the number, I'll definitely phone him. How would it be if I gave him a gift?'

'You can decide what you want to do. I prefer not to say anything.'

'Right. Let me tell you what I asked your permission for.'

'Tell me.'

'You can use my car, can't you? I hardly get the time nowadays. And I'm going to be away for a month. If you use it, the engine will remain in good condition.'

'No, don't make such requests.'

'Rohini is close to you that's why you live in her flat. But I'm no one, isn't it?'

'It's because I can afford to pay a part of the monthly instalment for Rohini's flat that I live here. If I hadn't been able to do that, I would have left long ago.'

'There's no instalment angle as far as my car is concerned. But you can pay me a rent for it.'

'Why should I pay a rent for your car for no reason? I'm planning to buy myself a small car.'

'Is that so? Great news! What car are you buying?'

'You won't like all that.'

'Why not?'

'Your career may be hindered if you even think of such a small car. For that matter, I can say emphatically that you won't even be agreeable to modelling for that car's advertisement.'

'Don't talk rubbish. Tell me what car you're buying.'

'A Maruti 800. Now tell me, will you model for that car?'

'I don't have much of a say regarding the products I model for or don't model for. My agency decides all that.'

'It's the same thing.'

'Forget about me. When are you getting your car?'

'Hold on! It's only at the planning stage. I need to be able to eat after paying the instalment for this flat.'

'When you get your car, you must take me for ice cream one day. Will you do that?'

'Only for ice cream? Fine. We'll go to "Naturals" on Napean

Sea Road. I love it.'

'Me too. But how about the "Naturals" outlet in Juhu?'

'We can go there.'

'I'll get to have a bit of a drive with you too.'

'But will it be appropriate for your career to be with me in a public place?'

'Please, don't pull my leg all the time. I have feelings too.'

'Hey, I'm not pulling your leg. I only said that keeping practical difficulties in mind. Rather, I'll order ice cream. That would be best, isn't it? And we could even sit on my balcony that day and have ice cream.'

'At last, you agreed to allow me into your balcony. That itself is a lot for me.'

'Don't speak too soon. It may be cancelled for all you know.'

'Please, please… Which cigarette do you like to smoke the most?'

'Why do you ask?'

'Is there a reason for everything? Can't one want to know something just like that, without any reason?'

'Just accept you don't know it.'

'It seems as soon as you step out of your limits, you shrink back inside again. Tell me, our ancestors were creatures with tails, but did yours have shells?'

'I probably had no ancestors at all. That's why I consider myself so rootless.'

'Tell me, do you think your roots are somewhere undersea?'

'Why do you ask?'

'Since you love the sea so much. You can spend the whole day filling your eyes with the sea.'

'That's a nice expression, "filling your eyes with the sea"!'

'Actually, that's pinched from Rudra's poem.'

'Perhaps it's a line from Shounak's book *Days and Nights*.'

'Wow, you got it right! Shounak is also a great admirer of yours. Do you know that?'

'No, I don't know anything.'

'When you say that you don't know anything, I wonder why I think that you say that because you know so much.'

'Don't always interpret me in your own way. It'll only leave you more confused, not less.'

'Tell me, Tinni, did you complete your school and college in Calcutta?'

'What does the database of your homework say?'

'Don't be like that. Please tell me.'

'I've heard that we lived in Darjeeling for some time when I was very small. But I don't remember that. After that, I went to school in Balurghat. College and university were in Calcutta.'

'Did you complete your PhD while working?'

'Yes.'

'Do you like literature?'

'Until a particular point of time, I loved it. Now I like it.'

'Why do you say that?'

'Perhaps a kind of inward detachment is created, when something that one loves becomes a subject that is taught every day . One often has to explain something to students in such a way that your own likes get wounded. But there's nothing to be done. Ensuring that they pass the examinations is the prime concern. It hardly has anything to do with my likes and dislikes.'

'I'll stand on your balcony and smoke a cigarette when you go for your shower now.'

'Ta ta, it's very late. I should have finished my shower by now. You're holding me up with words. That's not good. The everyday routine that I have constructed for myself is getting derailed. It'll be difficult for me to be alone.'

'Do you mean that? Will you miss me, Tinni?'

'I won't miss you. It's just that once I get used to talking, I'll find it difficult later. Solitude will become difficult.'

'So shall I cancel my travel programme?'

'Why should you do that?'

'Because you said you'll find it difficult.'

'That's not what I said.'

'Rohini told me repeatedly that you shouldn't be inconvenienced in any way. That's the first and most fundamental condition for my staying in this place.'

'That's why you shouldn't talk to me at all, other than what's absolutely necessary.'

'It's not in my nature to say anything more than what's necessary, either. But talking to you has become absolutely vital for me. Please try to understand that.'

'It's best not to try to apply the simple formula that just because Leena liked me, you must too.'

'How did Leena come into the picture?'

'It's you who said that it was only after hearing from Leena that your interest in me increased.'

'It's not that; you could say my fear regarding you was reduced a bit. If you had behaved sternly with Leena that day, then perhaps this morning would have come a year later.'

'It seems that if I had told off Leena, I would not have lost my sleep today.'

'You can sleep for as long as you like from tomorrow.'

'Why from tomorrow? I'll go to sleep after lunch today and only wake up tomorrow morning.'

'My flight is at dawn tomorrow. I'll leave by 3 a.m. You can go to sleep then. Don't object. No one will bother you like this for a month.'

'Have you finished packing?'

'That's always more or less ready. Besides, thanks to you and Raju, all my things are so well organized.'

'But I too have to get ready for college.'

'What time is your class tomorrow?'

'At 12.'

'You can sleep from 3 to 10 in the morning. You can get up after that, have a shower, eat today's leftovers, and go to college.'

'And what about preparing for my lecture?'

'That's not a big deal for you, is it?'

'What do you mean?'

'I mean, it's your own subject, all very simple for you.'

'Not at all, sir. I have to spend quite a few hours every day preparing for what I have to teach.'

'So that means you are still a student? Of course, I used to see my Ma too doing her studies every day, as a rule. Even if she didn't sit at her desk, she always carried a book to the bedroom.'

'What was your Ma's subject?'

'History. And you know, I used to get high marks in history! Ma used to teach me. She used to write out the answers. And she used to say, see how interesting it is—whatever happened in the past is happening again today, and will also happen in the future. There's only some outward change. But the inner essence stays the same. The same notion of a constant is at work in science too. All change is only outward. What does your literature say?'

'It says a lot. How much do I know? But perhaps a similarity with your views can be found in many aspects.'

'Go and have your shower. Come back to a new incarnation. Do you sing in the bathroom?'

'Not always.'

'I sing in the bathroom because I lack the courage to sing at other times.'

'Who's ringing the bell at this time?'

'Let me attend to that. Go for your shower.'

Chapter 3

'You! Why suddenly, and without any prior intimation?'

'Did I disturb you?'

'No.'

'Don't be stressed. Your flight is at dawn. I'll just check if your luggage is alright and leave. Who's in the bedroom?'

'There's no one.'

'Then how come you were taken aback to see me? I was wondering whether my girlfriend also visits you nowadays! What's up? Tell me!'

'Nothing's up. I don't have a good feeling at all about this tour.'

'Listen, 75% of the money has been credited into your account. The rest will come in due course. And I've told them that they have to pay extra if there's any time overrun.'

'I'm not worried about the money. I'm thinking about all that has to be done.'

'Leave that to me. I'll inform you in time. I'll be with you throughout the tour. There's nothing for you to be worried about.'

'What if, like last time, you have some work in between?'

'I didn't have any work in between last time. My son fell ill.'

'Good. Take care of everything here before you leave.'

'Yes. Do you want to go and see the house in Juhu today?'

'No. I'll do whatever has to be done after I return. You don't have to tell anyone else about all that.'

'Make sure you sign the cheques for this flat before you leave.'

'Thanks for reminding me about that, let me do that now.'

'Listen, I have to go. Are you coming to the party? Leena wanted to know.'

'No, I'm not coming. Tell Leena I'll be sleeping. I'll phone her once I reach the airport. When does her shooting start?'

'In the next two weeks. Okay. Bye. Take care. The car will be here by 3 a.m.'

'Of course, I know I have to leave at 3 a.m.'

'I didn't ask you what you're doing for your meals today.'

'I'll make something or the other. Thanks for your concern.'

'Okay. See you there. At the airport. Don't forget to take your medicines.'

'Bye.'

Chapter 4

'Was it your assistant?'

'Do you know him?'

'No. But he comes from time to time and asks me whether any papers have arrived for you. He's very diligent in taking care of your affairs.'

'Yes. Actually, Suraj is a close friend. If even a single rupee due to me isn't received on time, he becomes terribly restless. He does my personal work of his own accord, although that's not part of his work. Perhaps the entire credit for the fact that I have wonderful communication with my folks at home goes to Suraj. Regular phone calls, sending emails to my parents, remembering to send gifts to Shreya on all occasions—unless Suraj was around, none of that would happen.'

'Yes, he remembers your medicines too.'

'I have no option but to pay heed to my doctor's advice. It's a matter of terrifying rules. Do you think so much physical work would be possible with an erratic lifestyle?'

'I don't know... Actually, I've never observed any celebrity from close quarters.'

'Why haven't you worn blue?'

'Which blue shall I wear, tell me? I couldn't figure out whether it's the sky or the sea that would be appropriate, that's why.'

'Whatever you might say, you look great in yellow too. Leena was right. Your dress sense is fantastic.'

'How are you doing with the pomfret?'

'Oh, it's getting along fine. I've only managed to marinate it so far. Let me prepare the coconut chutney. And then it'll be done in no time. Will you help me a bit? Please dice some potatoes for the *alu bhaja*. I'll serve you crispy *alu bhaja,* just like "Oh Calcutta"!'

'And did the *alu posto* get buried?'

'No, no, not at all. I'll do that myself. If I invite you and then make you do a lot of work, you'll never accept my invitations. Or you'll invite me and get me to do a lot of work.'

'How much older than you is Shreya?'

'Exactly two years. Don't you have any siblings?'

'No. I'm an only child.'

'Do you know Leena is my first cousin?'

'Really! Was Leena in Bombay before you came here?'

'They grew up in Pune. Both my aunt and her husband are doctors settled in Pune. And Leena never thought of anything besides the film institute in Pune. She's a great singer of Indian classical music.'

'She never told me anything about herself.'

'Perhaps after talking to you, she thought that if she said too much in front of you, her image would be destroyed. Or maybe after spending a lot of time with people like us, she was unsure about how to present herself before a normal person like you.'

'So, Leena came to find out who her cousin was sharing a flat with.'

'You could say that.'

'So, were Leena's fears allayed?

'How does it matter to you what Leena thinks?'

'Hey, why me, she's your cousin, so it does matter to you.'

'No, it's nothing to me either.'

'Okay, it's nothing to you either. Would you like to have fruit punch? But I'll make it.'

'Great! May I smoke a cigarette in the kitchen?'

'Is it really necessary?'

'No, it's not necessary. But it may enhance my enjoyment.'

'When did you go home last?'

'During Diwali... And you?'

'I don't have a home anymore. I'm homeless.'

'What do you mean by homeless?

'Without roots. Rootless. I have no home. I have no city.'

'Why? Don't you consider Bombay to be your own city?'

'Not entirely yet. Perhaps, if I can stay longer here, I'll think so.'

'If you can stay, why do you say that? Are you planning to shift somewhere else?'

'I don't plan anymore now because not a single plan has materialized in my life so far. I want to move with the times. Let's see where I end up.'

'You said you wanted to live in Pondicherry after you retire.'

'Oh, I've had so many wishes from the time I was a child. And so many times have I gone far away from that and run after a different kind of signal in order to survive...'

'What did you want to become when you were a child?'

'A doctor.'

'Didn't you try?'

'After I grew up a bit, I thought it would be good to become a journalist. By then, I had started writing a bit.'

'Why did you change that?'

'There are lots of inconveniences when one grows up in a

small mofussil town. Openings are few. The competition is a lot less. One doesn't develop a professional outlook like girls and boys living in big cities do. It isn't always possible to figure out one's own position in the larger context of the changing world.'

'When did you decide to become a teacher?'

'You could say it was after I went to Calcutta to join college. It was a kind of intoxication—from Calcutta, college, College Street...'

'You decided to teach in college. But you used to teach at a university back in Calcutta, didn't you?'

'That was another chapter in my life.'

'About which you cast words into the sea now?'

'I don't know.'

'You know it all. Just for today, please don't consider me to be like the sea. Give me something. I give you my word; I won't be indifferent.'

'Does anyone decide to be indifferent? And yet, one doesn't realize when things go awry. Do you like kokum?'

'Why?'

'Then I'll add a little bit to the fruit punch.'

'Please go ahead with your recipe. I'm sure I'll enjoy that.'

'Did you have the hilsa fish the other day?'

'Arey, I had left a note thanking you! Did you find it? Suraj had signed on that too; did you see it?'

'I didn't know that both of you would be there, or else I would have left some more.'

'There was plenty. I had planned to make jeera rice. Suraj said that unless it was plain basmati rice, it wouldn't go well with the fish. He made the rice. You made it with mustard sauce, didn't you?'

'Not mustard sauce. It was made with freshly ground mustard seeds.

'White mustard seeds?'

'I used white and black seeds in equal proportion. And also, a teaspoon of poppy seeds, green chilies, and salt, all ground together.'

'Did you use the microwave?'

'Yes. Because that's convenient. My Ma used to put it in a container and steam it with the rice being cooked, or in the pressure cooker.'

'Tinni, do you know how to make *payesh*?'

'No, I don't know.'

'It's clear from your face that you aren't telling the truth.'

'Maybe so.'

'Why did you reply in that way?'

'If I said I know, and then if you ask me to make it even by mistake, I'd be in deep trouble.'

'What trouble?'

'I'll have to remember what you said, prepare *payesh*, and treat you to it someday. Or if I ever prepare it, just like that, I'll want to treat you to it. I'll remember you even if you aren't here; I'll want to keep it for you, and so on and so forth…'

'Even if all that really happens, what's the harm in that?'

'What's to be gained either? I don't want to entangle my life anymore with anyone else's likes or dislikes, or with waiting, expectation, or anything like that.'

'Why do you keep aside a share of your food for me from time to time?'

'Maybe that's because you don't have any demands. Or maybe it's because you leave something for me from time to time that I thought I too should have the decency to reciprocate. Nothing more than that. And that's why I wasn't bothered at all about whether you ate it or some other guest of yours ate it. I didn't have to worry about whether you liked it or disliked it either.'

'By the way, did you eat the few things I had left for you? Or did you give it to someone else? I hope you didn't throw it away! I'll be very sad in that case. I was really waiting for you to say, "Dev, you've done an excellent job!'"

'Didn't I tell you? Sorry, sorry. But I did tell you over the phone once that your methi-chicken was great.'

'And the keema-paratha?'

'That was very nice too. But I ate it over three days. The parathas were extremely heavy.'

'What about the biryani?'

'Do I have to say everything today?'

'Fine. I'm really keen to get the opportunity to have informal conversations with you. Please don't change your mind all of a sudden!'

'I'll learn to cook biryani from you one day.'

'But there'll be a fee.'

'Tell me what you want to charge?'

'You tell me what you can pay. If you leave it entirely to me, there's the possibility of you going bankrupt.'

'Find out from the internet about the financial capability of a senior teacher, and prepare your bill accordingly.'

'Okay.'

'How long will you microwave the pomfret?'

'I think I'll microwave it for four minutes and then grill it a bit. It'll turn out crispy then. I like that crispiness.'

'Go and wash your hands.'

'Is your drink ready?'

'Yes sir.'

'Okay, let's say cheers!'

'Cheers!'

'You were tired; you needed to sleep. Please don't be angry with me.'

'Do you really think I'm angry?'

'Every now and then you become strangely serious. I get scared and don't feel at ease.'

'Not for once do I think that you're afraid of me, even the slightest bit—quite the opposite, in fact.'

'Meaning, you're afraid of me.'

'I didn't say that. You're going out of your way on my behalf.'

'When did I go out of my way?'

'You did. Maybe because your likes are mixed up with that, you don't realize its intensity. Or you don't want to.'

'I don't think so much about what I do, believe me. I do whatever comes to mind. Even the things I've told you, or whatever I've been doing, are in no way calculated. It's spontaneous. And if you really find it painful, then I give you my word that I'll never express any wish of mine in this way before you. It's only today that's completely different. Let it be different.'

'Actually, I want to say something and end up saying something else. I'm not in the habit of sharing my personal matters with anyone for a very long time; that's why I make a mess of it.'

'I get so many opportunities to flirt that I don't have to wait for that. And love—a lot of experience in that too.'

'After Sumedha?'

'I had a great relationship with my classmate in Delhi, Anandi.'

'Wow! Your lovers' names are great!'

'The name Achira, too, is extremely uncommon. But Tinni is even sweeter than that.'

'I was talking about the names of your lovers.'

'I'm talking about them too.'

'I warn you, don't try to pull my leg.'

'I swear, I'm not pulling your leg. Perhaps the inference that I'm your lover is not correct, but I do not doubt at all the fact that I love you.'

'Let's change the topic. How about listening to some music?'

'No, I only want to hear about you now and nothing else.'

'I don't have all that much to say that I can tell you that all day.'

'Why should it be only about you? I too have lots and lots to tell you.'

'All rubbish.'

'Rubbish things, nice things, lots of things. I'm happy to listen more and say little.'

'Listen, Dev, is there any chance of meeting Rohini this time?'

'Maybe. I'll visit Shreya for two or three days. She told me she'd call Rohini and Samir over then. But why do you ask?'

'I had asked Rohini to pick up something in Venice. She told me that if she met you, she'd send it through you.'

'What's that?'

'A tiny crystal dolphin.'

'Do you like crystals? I'm going to Venice; I'll get it for you. Shall I get you a pendant? It'll look fabulous. A small one. Which sparkles.'

'But I don't wear any jewelry like that.'

'You don't wear it, but you will. Your pearls are fabulous.'

'Which one?'

'The one you wear on your ear.'

'How do you observe so much? And how do you know about it?'

'After all, the number of lovers ever since my childhood is not at all small. If I couldn't learn even this little bit…'

'I suppose your lovers made you into a jewelry design specialist?'

'Instead of "specialist", you could say connoisseur. Look, when I gaze at my lover, it's vital to observe her entirely. Surely, you'd agree with that?'

'Who knows… I don't know.'

'You can't just say, "I don't know". You too had a love affair with Shubhro for several years, didn't you?'

'You know so many things about me.'

'If you had the slightest interest in me, you would also have known plenty of things about me.'

'Who knows. Actually, I have no desire to know everything about anyone at all.'

'But Shubhro was not your classmate. Were you the same age?'

'You could say that.'

'What do you mean by "You could say that"?'

'I mean, both of us completed secondary and higher secondary school in the same year.'

'He is an IIT-ian.'

'You know everything. Would it be a great loss if you refrained from asking me about all this?'

'Does it hurt you a lot when any discussion regarding Shubhro arises?'

'You don't know Shubhro. You don't know anything about him, so I don't understand why you need to discuss him.'

'Why are you getting angry? I want to know about you. So obviously, the people whose names arise or are involved with you will be discussed. That's all. And why be so touchy about Shubhro?'

'Let me decide who I'll be whatever with. I can't let anyone else do all that. And it's because I don't like to talk about such things that I like to stay alone. I don't have the slightest inclination to sit with someone and discuss the merits and demerits of someone else.'

'Tinni, have you decided that you'll give me a piece of your mind at the slightest pretext?'

'No.'

'Then, why are you getting so angry?'

'You want to discuss things about me that are painful, like a bloody wound. I have thrown all that away into the sea.'

'But it was you who said that the sea doesn't keep anything—that it returns everything. So, what's the use of throwing it into the sea? Tinni, look me in the eye. Give me some of it, and you'll see that a lot comes back transformed. Everything becomes saltier in the sea. Maybe I'll change it somewhat by polarizing it. Believe me. I'm not flirting. Please give me something. The burden of your pain. Don't be so silent. Please talk to me. For the sake of your yellow sari, talk to me.'

'I'm perfectly fine by myself. Believe me. There's no void within me. I have no demands at all from life. Having this personal time for myself is vital for me.'

'I know that. But life is not just for whiling away like this by gazing at the sea.'

'So, what's to be done with one's life? It's a game of dice. In which sometimes this person loses and sometimes the other, isn't it? One defeat of mine was so severe that I have no strength left to challenge that.'

'Who said that you've lost, Tinni? Relationships mean that whether it's defeat or victory, it happens to both people involved.'

'By the way, did Rohini give you the responsibility for counselling behind my back?'

'Why do you ask me that?'

'Rohini told me, "Dev hardly talks at all. He's always very concerned about his career. Don't worry, he won't go out of his way to communicate with you."'

'Didn't she say anything else?'

'Yes, she said a lot more. She said that you lead a high-profile life. That you have a girlfriend, etcetera, etcetera.'

'Not just having a girlfriend, but being with lots and lots of women, she must have said that.'

'Rohini didn't tell me all that. And it's not as if Rohini and I were busy sitting and discussing thousands of tales regarding your life.'

'You people should have thought about the fact that you would have to live in the same flat as me, at least for some time.'

'That's true. But do you realize that the fact that you're famous was very useful for us in that regard?'

'No, I don't realize anything. Listen, the cooking's almost done. Let's sit on your balcony and have coffee.'

'Another volley of questions awaits me once again, doesn't it?'

'Alright, I won't ask any questions. But you have to give me your word that you'll believe everything I say.'

'Why, what are you going to say that there's a possibility I might not believe you?'

'I don't know. After all, I don't have a script before me. I'll say whatever comes to my mind.'

'Tell me about Anandi.'

'It's been five years since I last saw the person you're asking about. But I'm not angry. Because I got whatever I had to from Anandi.'

'What do you mean?'

'Meaning, I was with her through the four years of college. And then, even after coming to Bombay, we were in close touch for a year. She then got a job in Bangalore. Whenever she had the time, she used to come to Bombay, and I too used to go to meet her. But I was still very anxious about my career. I was not in a position or frame of mind to get married at the time. Anandi was planning to get married and go away to the U.S. I didn't want to do that. I realized that if one forced someone, the outcome would eventually not be good. I'll show you Anandi's picture. She's beautiful. Gorgeous, intelligent.'

'Do you know where Anandi is now?'

'She phones me every now and then and imparts wisdom. She says, "Dev, it's high time. Get married," and so on. You know, I was telling Anandi about you the other day.'

'About me?'

'Yes, about you.'

'That's what I want to know; what exactly about me?'

'That I share a flat with you, and that you're impossibly beautiful. Impossibly stubborn. That you don't have the slightest interest in paying attention to me. About all that.'

'Everything you just said is like Amit in *Shesher Kobita*. Which is true only for the moment. And that's why I'm not getting too perturbed. Actually, this will also be a test of how much I've attained through my *tapasya*.'

'Tinni, do you agree that no person's entire life is a science laboratory?'

'I didn't get you.'

'I doubt if there's even a single person in India as knowledgeable as you, and yet you say that you can't understand.'

'I really couldn't understand.'

'That means you agree that a lot of things in this world are still beyond your comprehension. So, it's wise not to be so vain as to think that you fully understand yourself too.'

'You know, at various times in my life, I've heard such contrary opinions about my intelligence that I really don't know what I ought to do to prove that I am intelligent.'

'Where's the need for you to prove anything?'

'You're the one who was trying to teach me what's wise.'

'Oh! I apologize if you're offended. Actually, you know, Tinni, I've not seen you laughing freely even once, that's why I look for various kinds of pretexts to see you cracking up in laughter.'

'Just stop doing research about me, and you'll see that you're in peace.'

'Who said I'm not in peace? I want to create a space within your silence. Can you grant me that? When Anandi actually told me one day about her marriage, do you know, at that moment I thought she was joking with me. After that, she really got married one day and went away. She was no longer mine. At the time, my external battles were so fierce that I didn't even get the respite to sit down alone and commune with myself about that. Only Suraj sensed something. He managed to get me a day's break on the pretext that I was down with fever. I drank all day and night in Suraj's flat itself; I wept my heart out and I also hurled some abuses at Anandi. After that, I fell asleep. When I woke up in the morning, I asked myself why I was so angry with Anandi. After all, she hadn't left me intentionally. She had a survival plan that couldn't be reconciled with my way of survival. Or one could say that I, too, couldn't accommodate her. And so there was no point in being angry with her. After all, we hadn't quarreled, or fought with each other. Both of us had decided that we ought to lead separate lives. But doesn't it hurt somewhere? Wasn't it painful? It still is.'

'The story of my life is entirely different from yours.'

'That's how it should be. After all, you're Tinni, and I'm Dev.'

'You're right.'

'I'm always right.'

'Your confidence is unprecedented!'

'I know that too. That's why I'm able to sit so close to you and talk to you. So many times, I thought that I'd tell you. And then it occurred to me that you might think that I'm taking advantage of the fact that we share a flat.'

'You're definitely doing that.'

'No, please, there's no point in viewing me like that.'

'But if we didn't have to share a flat, I would never have even met a person like you.'

'Why?'

'There would have been no opportunity to get acquainted with a person like you. And I don't go out of my way and try to get acquainted with anyone.'

'Look, someone or another has to make the introduction. Whether that's by going out of the way or by creating an attraction through one's entire presence.'

'I don't want to talk to you.'

'Please, please, Tinni, Achira, the sea's blue, don't be angry.'

'Just shut up.'

'Alright, I won't talk anymore. You talk now. I didn't realize from afar that you can get so angry. I had thought you could only say charming things and look with a hint of a smile in your eyes.'

'You don't have to say anymore.'

'No, there's something else that you're very good at—that's muttering to yourself.'

'Absolutely not, I don't mutter. I do talk to myself quite loudly sometimes.'

'Actually, I have to observe everything furtively from afar. And for that matter, how many days in all have I been here? It was you who calculated and said that it was probably less than a month and a half.'

'If I had known that you were following me like this, I would definitely have been a bit more careful.'

'What would you have done? You would have sat all alone on the balcony, singing with tears streaming down from your eyes.'

'But all that's my personal business. No one should have the right to intervene in that.'

'Perhaps they really shouldn't. But I too won't be able to make you understand, logically, why I started thinking so much. Time and again, I've felt that my world is such that when I carry that along, I can reach almost no one, or, one could say, any one's doorstep. That's why you too consider all I say to be mere dialogue.'

'Believe me, I don't think about any of that. I've seen such astonishing aspects of people's behavior that I now know that everything's possible in this world. I've limited my personal demands from this probable world to only a small circle. It's necessary for me to stay afar so that no tangent can intersect that.'

'A tangent doesn't merely intersect, Tinni. It can also just touch the circle. And the characteristics of the circle are not destroyed because of that.'

'As soon as you hear something or get a word, it's as if you've received a pass and at once scored a goal.'

'Did you speak to Rohini yesterday?'

'How did you know about that?'

'Obviously from Rohini. It's your birthday tomorrow; I wanted to postpone my travel by a day. But it just wasn't possible. So, we'll have an early celebration of your birthday today.'

'I stopped celebrating my birthday several years ago.'

'But Rohini told me that you used to celebrate it without using the word birthday. She suggested the same to me too. But I'm also like you in all respects. I don't like it if I can't do it in my own way.'

'Let's hear what your own way is.'

'You've been hearing that since this morning. And you have to hear it until three in the morning tomorrow. Will you go to the airport to see me off?'

'No.'

'You have an immense vocabulary of monosyllables, don't you? Who bought you this sari?

'I bought it.'

'May I buy you a sari?'

'No.'

'Why not?'

'Because I said so.'

'Would you have objected if Rohini gave it to you?'

'Perhaps not.'

'So, you are objecting because it's me?'

'Yes.'

'Fine, when you don't have any objection, I'll buy many saris all at once and give them to you.'

'Let's see.'

'Do see!'

'When you sit in the corner of the balcony, you look like a stone figure, like a piece of sculpture placed there.'

'Tell me where you can see that from.'

'All angles can't be revealed to you just now. You look great when you move about in the kitchen too.'

'Men love to watch women moving about in the kitchen and cooking.'

'I haven't seen too many women in the kitchen. Not my Ma. Not my friends either. I've seen the maid-servant sometimes.'

'You don't spare even her.'

'Damn! When I saw you, it seemed like you were working in a studio. After all, I love cooking, but everything turns out lousy. But out of fear of you, I don't leave without finally cleaning up.'

'At least you have this fear.'

'I used to.'

'No, you'll fear in future too.'

'I won't fear. I'll use the kitchen beautifully like you. When I stay here, I'll cook for you too.'

'You don't have to be so solicitous. I can't cook for you every day when you're here, so don't put me under any obligation by doing that.'

'There's so much I can do for you.'

'No, you don't have to do anything.'

'Why, that time, some days back, didn't I bring down a container for you from a kitchen shelf?'

'Playing the fool again. I'm telling you, once this conversation ends, it won't begin again. Who's that, at this time?'

'See, you too don't want anyone else to come now. That means you're enjoying talking to me. But you won't admit it. You think that would be a defeat for you. Add the joy of your own victory to someone else's victory, and you'll see the pain gets reduced considerably.'

'Can you see who's at the door? It must be your guest.'

'I'm not in the mood now. You go and open the door. If they ask for me, say I'm not there. And that you don't know when I'll be back.'

'Don't tutor and send me like dads do with kids. I might mess it up.'

'Please go. Let me sit in a pose like yours and see how it feels.'

'You have a lot of thrashing in your fate.'

'Only in my fate?'

'Wait, I'll just be back.'

Chapter 5

'What's this?'

'Flowers.'

'I can see it's flowers; where was the need to do all this?'

'It's your birthday, so can't I even give you some flowers?'

'You could have brought one or two yourself. But so many? And through a florist, there's no point in doing all this.'

'Please stop looking for the point in everything in life.'

'So, everything ought to happen just like that, is it?'

'Yes, what's the harm in that? Can't I do this for your birthday?'

'Has anyone made you vow that you must do it?'

'Still… I'll feel bad about it. If I can't celebrate it the way you did. I'll view myself poorly.'

'Why's that?'

'You know it. But hey, you're the one who said that you don't really think about my profession, etcetera. So, where does all this talk come from?

'I don't know. You could have skipped all this.'

'I did it because I couldn't skip it. Getting you some flowers that you like. Please don't get angry about such a trivial matter.'

'You've uttered a million "pleases" already since morning; don't say it anymore.'

'Alright, I won't. Please come and sit here.'

'There you go again.'

'Alright, I'm not going to say "please". Come here. Do I have to invite you into your own balcony?'

'But you came and sat here without invitation.'

'One has to be forceful in some matters.'

'Meaning?'

'Meaning, fold your knees and sit here like a little girl. What's the number of your lipstick?'

'Which lipstick?'

'The one you have on now?'

'Now? Am I wearing lipstick? Is your eyesight failing you in the daytime? Get your eyes checked. After all, you won't be able to wear spectacles, so get contact lenses.'

'Ha, you don't even know that I've been wearing lenses for a long time. My fans know all that. But you don't know anything even after being here for two years.'

'What do you mean by "being here"?'

'I mean even after sharing a flat.'

'You also don't know that I don't wear lipstick.'

'So what? Shall I touch once and see whether you actually have lipstick on or not?'

'You're getting too big for your boots, aren't you?'

'No, too small. You didn't say whether you liked the flowers. You only scolded me.'

'I liked it.'

'You said it as if a gun was held at your head.'

'Of course, it's a bit like that. After Anandi, who were you in love with?'

'With Tinni.'

'Don't talk rubbish.'

'Arey, why should it be rubbish? It's true. You find it somewhat abnormal to hear that. Yet it's true. And before that, I'd gone around with quite a few people. One could say they were more than friends.'

'Were they people from your world?'

'But you too are from my world, Tinni.'

'No, that's completely wrong. Perhaps it's because I don't fit in your world that you're attracted to me. Anyway, once you talk some more to me, I'm sure this enchantment of yours will come to an end.'

'How much you know!'

'I know myself.'

'I don't know myself at all. Is it correct to think like that?'

'This time, wherever you go, if you get the time, do bring me some photos of the landscape there.'

'Only photos?'

'Yes. Only photos.'

'I'll send you one every day by email.'

'No, no, you don't have to do that since you'll be terribly busy. It's fine if you bring it back with you. And if you're unable to take the pictures yourself, you can buy some postcards and bring me those.'

'And the crystal dolphin from Venice. Will you talk to me for a little while over the phone every day? Tell me what time is convenient for you, so I can call.'

'All times are convenient for me, but then again, all times are inconvenient too.'

'In that case, I'll call you whenever I get the time. Can you call Raju once more after I've gone and have him tidy up my room?'

'Why? Didn't you say that you hadn't messed up the room?'

'That's right, but still, take a look once.'

'I feel terribly uncomfortable entering someone else's room. Why don't you tell Suraj so he can send someone over?'

'Okay, you don't have to do anything. Don't bother about it. You don't have to offer any suggestions about it either.'

'See, how you got angry! That's what I object to. Don't expand your thoughts, as far as I'm concerned. This is the kind of person I am. The more you think of me, the more you'll be pained. I've wasted a lot of time in my life on others, over their likes and dislikes, so much so that there's hardly anything I can call my own. That's why I desperately want to retreat into myself.'

'Stay the way you are. If I come in the way of how you want to be, protest at once. I'll mend my ways. Don't be troubled. And definitely not on my account. Or anyone else's… If you can think of me as a friend, that's enough for me. You don't have to be bothered about what I might think about you.'

'So, a person ought to be bothered about another person, is it? Nothing else?'

'Listen, whatever it may be, you should stay well. Get out of the grip of your anguish. Why should your beautiful eyes only be full of tears? Let there be the light of joy in them.'

'Those tears have made me who I am today. Do you know that? The Achira whom you like, even a bit, has been formed by those feelings of agony and a history of anguish.'

'Who doesn't have a history of anguish? And does that mean one should go on holding on to that? The person I am today was created by my loving Anandi and being indulged in by her. If I use that to erode myself because I don't have her, wouldn't that amount to insulting her essence?'

'Do you love Anandi very much? Would you ever be able to love someone else again in the same way?'

'A person doesn't spend even two consecutive days in exactly the same way, so how can it be possible with love? Maybe I'll love more. Love in another way. I'll want more. I'll want to fill up the gaps that were evident in the relationship with her.'

'Who knows… I can't think as you do yet.'

'Don't worry yourself trying. Move along in your own way, but listen to the sounds wafting in with the breeze. You'll see that life is not a game of dice. Don't be anguished. Remember, tears heal you.'

'Theory of catharsis.'

'That's the problem with theorists like you. You can't be at peace unless you give everything a label. My Ma was like that. She used to theorize even about my wanting to eat chocolate.'

'Is there a lot of resemblance between your Ma and me?'

'Why? You'll tell me next that all men want to find their mothers in women, etcetera, etcetera.'

'I won't say anything. It's alright. Don't scold me anymore. Please.'

'Don't lean so much!'

'So what? Will I fall down? I could have fallen long ago. At first, that's what I thought was the means to escape from my blackhole. But later, I realized Rohini would get involved in a lot of trouble on my account. I was only thinking of myself; I was selfish. Right from bringing me over to Bombay to finding me a job and getting me a place to stay, Rohini did all that, and there was no self-interest in any of that. In fact, it was because of me that her marriage to Samir was postponed for more than a year. She wouldn't leave Bombay until I got better. Samir didn't take that well, and I didn't want to be involved unnecessarily in those troubles of theirs. And now, like you, I have to think of my public face. So don't worry. I won't fall.'

'Tinni, you have nice hair. Why do you always tie up such beautiful long hair?'

'I guess it has to be tied up because it's long. I'm thinking of cutting it very short. There won't be any more of all the trouble of washing and tying and so on.'

'Please let it loose, just once. Let me see.'

'Why? Are you a beauty contest judge?'

'Are you a contestant? In that case, you've already won, hands down. There's no need for any new contest. Untie the knot, please.'

'Again, "please". If only you knew what the sea breeze does to this long hair.'

'What happens?'

'What else? A complete mess.'

'Okay. One day, I'll make the mess.'

'No way.'

'Just you wait!'

'I'll cut it before that.'

'By the way, the style in which you tie your hair when you're home, what's that called?'

'It's no style. It's just a *khonpa*, what's called a chignon.'

'Wow! The name's great!'

'Leena said she'll learn that too from me.'

'But she has only medium-length hair. Can it be done with that?'

'Yes, it can. Did Anandi have long hair?'

'No, she had a blunt cut earlier, and a wedge haircut afterwards.'

'I'm planning to get a mushroom cut.'

'You still have thick hair. You can cut it once it gets thin.'

'No, I have to spend a lot of time on this hair. And I don't have much time. I don't even have enough time for my reading nowadays.'

'Just stop muttering in the balcony, and you'll manage just fine.'

'Wow! Now you're bossing me around!'

'What can one do if you behave like a child?'

'Listen, tell the man whom Suraj sends for bill payments to come next week. It's the last date for paying the Corporation tax.'

'Okay. I'll tell him just now. His contact number is in the diary in the drawing room. He'll come in time. If there is a delay, please give him a call. Hey, he can also handle your car documents. Wait; let me talk to him.'

'Will he charge a lot?'

'Why?'

'I mean, because he does your work. Those who work for people like you charge so much that if it's imposed on me, it may turn out that the brokerage fee is greater than the price of the car.'

'You're crazy…'

'I'm stating facts. You have no idea because you don't know about such things. Suraj handles everything. You don't realize what's involved.'

'Hey, Suraj informs me about all expenses and so on, alright? Do you think I just float along in the air? If that were the case, I wouldn't have to earn a living. I have to think of the future as well.'

'Why? You can join your Baba's business then.'

'Do you think my Baba will wait all his life for me?'

'Yes, of course. That's what parents do.'

'You're saying this?'

'Leave me out of it.'

'Why?'

'My Baba was not a businessman like yours.'

'But he knows all about the business of life, in his own way.'

'Look, if we can get along without such discussions on personal matters, where's the need for that?'

'The coffee's finished. What will we have now? Some vodka?'

'No.'

'Alright. You needn't say no so gravely. Is it written somewhere that professors are not supposed to drink?'

'Neither is it written anywhere that they must drink.'

'Alright, how about some iced tea?'

'That's a good idea. Wait, I have some special Nilgiri tea. A student of mine gave it to me. They have a tea-garden in Ooty. I never tried it. Let's try that today.'

'Soak the tea then. I'll be back from my room in a couple of minutes.'

'Okay.'

Chapter 6

I have to discipline myself more strictly. Why am I talking so much all of a sudden? I haven't yet been able to come to terms with myself. I shouldn't be talking to anyone. Is it true that after Rohini left, another void was created within me? I'm supposed to sort out my inner matters. Why should I talk to anyone else? Or does one at all need to talk? That's why I write so that I can express my concerns in my own way. No, there's no way I can talk any more. Talking is very dangerous. Perhaps I have to escape from here too now. But where will I go? Am I gradually becoming mad with all these complications of mine?

'There you go muttering again.'

'Oh! You're back? The tea's ready.'

'Not here, let's sit on the balcony.'

'No, you have the tea. I'll finish something quickly and be back.'

'What happened now?'

'Why? Nothing's happened.'

'You want to escape?'

'Escape? Why? Where to? And from whom?'

'From yourself. But Tinni, running away from oneself is probably the most difficult thing.'

'That's what I want to do skillfully.'

'That means you know you're not being able to do it; that's why you try to build walls around yourself.'

'I can do it. You have no idea about this. Anyway, whether you do or don't, it's entirely my business.'

'Alright, do what you like; let's at least have the tea now.'

'You have it. I'll just change quickly and be back.'

'Why a change all of a sudden? I like this yellow sari of yours very much.'

'I don't like it.'

'So you'll force yourself to wear something else? Because I like it. Do that. I won't stop you. Do whatever you like. Do whatever makes you feel happy. Don't ever bother about other people's likes or dislikes.'

'No, I suddenly remembered that I was supposed to go to the British Council. In all the blabbering since morning, I forgot all about that.'

'To the library? Shall I drop you there?'

'No.'

'When will you be back?'

'In a couple of hours.'

'Alright, you do that. I'll complete the rest of the cooking. Let me think about how to arrange the table for you.'

'Are you testing your patience?'

'Why do you say that? When did you observe me to be impatient that you ask me this? I don't know if I'm very peaceful, but just like I don't suddenly get excited about anything, nothing makes me uncontrollable or restless either.'

'Don't defeat me, please. Don't defeat me.'

'Tinni, I have a lot of things to say to you. But this isn't the proper time. So, don't worry, I'll be there.'

'I have a *sadhana* of my own. If that's destroyed, my self-deception will be exposed. I've divided my time accordingly. I'm hardly able to recognize myself when that's blown away by some wind. My whole existence becomes agonizing.'

'Actually, Tinni, you think all the time that a single painful memory and its agony comprise your world, your existence.'

'It's not that. I can't make you understand. I don't have the capability to make you understand. My notion of life is entirely my own. I don't find any peace by following some life design I heard about or saw. But that's no one's fault. That sense of separation has penetrated into every atom of my being. That's why I can't get involved with anything. Perhaps this can't be discerned from outside. That's why some notions regarding me are created, which are not correct, or, one could say, those notions keep changing very frequently. I don't have any power to control the situation.'

'Forget about all that now, Tinni. Go to the library and be back. We can talk about all this later—some other day, if we get the time.'

'Actually, you know, even if I go to the library, I'll not really be able to do any work. My inner restlessness will spin me to death. I'll walk here and there and return tired. After that, I'll go to sleep.'

'Then don't go out now. Want to listen to some music? I have some trance music which is extremely soothing when one is agitated. Want to listen to that?'

'No.'

'Why not? Because I'm asking you to?'

'It's not that. I won't be able to make you understand.'

'You don't have to. Do whatever you feel like right now. Don't bother about anyone else.'

'But I myself don't know what exactly I'd like to do now. I don't know that.'

'That happens with everyone. You think that it only happens to you? You'll never be able to explain what's bothering you. But this kind of thing happens again and again to everyone. You know, Tinni, human life is something about which the moment for making the final pronouncement will never arrive. Everything is nascent. Everything is a mere hypothesis.'

'I think about all this every day. All my thinking becomes even more murky and salty with the waters of the sea and the salty breeze.'

'That's bound to happen, Tinni. After all, the elixir of life is meant for the gods. It's only salt that's the fate of humans.'

'Maybe that's why the wounds just don't heal at all.'

'That's why countless streams pour out from your eyes.'

'But still, peace eludes me.'

'What does peace look like? Is she as beautiful as you?'

'I warn you. You should think a little before sitting in front of a woman and making a comment like that.'

'Only a little? I thought about it two hundred times in this while. By the way, you ought to pay me interest for those additional thoughts.'

'Only interest?'

'Do you want to pay the principal as well?'

'I don't want anything.'

'Do you want to just stay silent and conceal the fire?'

'How did you know whether it's fire or ashes?'

'You teach texts, and that too to students, while I show life to all kinds of people.'

'Do you believe that all the characters you portray are real?'

'If this life of exile of yours is real, then all those cinema characters are even more true than reality.'

'This argument can go on for very long, but I'm not in the mood now.'

'What does Tinni's mood say?'

'I feel terribly restless. I realize that. I can't explain any more. The tea's gone completely cold.'

'Yes, don't have that now. It'll taste bitter.'

'You know so much.'

'Hey, what the heck? I'm trying to impress you.'

'How can one argue with you? I don't feel like solving any logical riddle right now.'

'Shut your eyes for a moment.'

'Why?'

'I want to see how your eyes will look with shadow.'

'What do you mean?'

'I was thinking about how you would look if you wore eye-shadow.'

'Why would I do that?'

'You don't have to do it; I only wanted to get an idea about how it would look.'

'Don't you have anything better to do.'

'No, I have nothing. Today's exclusively for Tinni.'

'But I didn't come to you with any demands; why are you suddenly so pleased with me?'

'Why can't you understand? All this is for my sake. Like God and a devotee.'

'Meaning?'

'The devotee thinks about God in so many ways. Such a lot of effort to please God, but does God have any use for any of that? It's of use only to the devotee.'

'Does God not serve any purpose at all?'

'Do you know what that purpose is?'

'I don't really know. But perhaps God can only prove himself through these efforts of devotees.'

'This devotee wishes for God to prove herself. Through the

devotee.'

'Neither am I God, nor you, my devotee. So, it's best not to carry on this debate.'

'Does God ever say that I am your God, and you are my devotee? It is the devotee who, through his faith and love, proves the existence of God.'

'A deeply philosophical discussion. I'm not competent enough for that.'

'Being confined to the limit of competence is nothing but sticking to an age-old habit. That's why man's soul cries for and seeks to reach the infinite. I'm sure it's clear what my own purpose is.'

'But how did I enter that world of your purpose?'

'You could say it's ordained by fate.'

'There's a lot I have to learn from you.'

'Do that.'

'No. I don't think that's possible any more. I'm getting old. My wishes can hardly advance two steps, they become weary.'

'Listen, if we don't eat now, I'll become weary too. And I won't be able to walk even two steps. And if I want to go to sleep here, would you be agreeable to that?'

'Come, let's eat.'

'Don't say that in such a gloomy way. I have been cooking for you since morning, and I have arranged the table all by myself so that when you eat, your eyes light up in pleasure. For the next one month, that image will keep...'

'Please, I'm an extremely ordinary person. My thinking is of an extremely ordinary kind. I live in someone else's house. If no other thought enters within that, I'll be able to survive. That's what I fear.'

'Why fear? How can a person—a person of flesh and blood—spend days, months, and years merely looking at her own darkness?'

'Why did you think it's darkness? There could be light too.'

'Definitely. But if any light at all percolated, you would have observed a deep affection.'

'And the one who is already sufficiently visible has no need for any external light.'

'It wouldn't be a wise thing for me to enter into a discussion with you about visibility. You understand philosophy much better than me; I know and accept that. Let's go to the dining table now.'

'You go. I'll come within two minutes.'

'Don't delay. I can't bear any more concealment today.'

'But I have a great need for concealment, or else all the wounds would be exposed. And that would be terribly shameful.'

'I'm famished, so if I become shameless, it'll be your responsibility to handle that.'

'I don't have any responsibilities. I discharged all my responsibilities a long time ago. I'm weightless, like a feather.'

'So, tell me now, how do you like the way I've arranged the table.'

'You're really very talented.'

'Are you teasing me?'

'Why would I tease you? That you can think of an insignificant, ordinary person like me and do so much despite all your fame, your preoccupations, and all the running around… Actually, I can hardly believe it. I think it's all a dream. I've never had a dream like this; that's why I can't get over my discomfort easily.'

'Just see, in the midst of all the talk, I forgot to bring enough serving spoons.'

'Sit down. I'll get it.'

'No, no, it's my day today. Let me do it today. I give you my word; I'll never ask you to do the same on my birthday.'

'Believe me, Dev, my…'

'What? Once more, please…'

'Once more what?'

'Call me by my name. Please, please…'

'You serve the rice. I'll bring the pickles.'

'Please get the chili flakes too, Tinni.'

'Your "pleases" are making me completely topsy-turvy.'

'Wow! That means you're still not completely distorted. I think I should be able to mend you if I apply a bit of my engineering skills.'

'I think the muttering has got you now.'

'Don't you like it? Just like an infectious disease, a feature of yours has entered me.'

'If it's a disease, it's best not to be exposed to it.'

'The pomfret looks fantastic. You're not saying anything; I'm having to praise my work by myself.'

'I'm a bit slow in all respects, that's missing in your homework; that's what your problem is.'

'No problem. Actually, I'm so tense that it's coming out in various ways.'

'Why are you tense? About the forthcoming tour? But that shouldn't be the case; after all, you're used to all this—the hard work, stardom... Is there tension even after reaching your position?'

'Do you know exactly where I've reached?'

'I don't know it all, but one doesn't have to make any effort to keep track of your fame and popularity. I only know that you've reached that kind of position.'

'Do you know Dev even a little bit?'

'I know that besides doing lots of things, you know how to cook. And now, after eating it, I'll be able to say how much of a specialist you are in cooking *patrani-machhi*.'

'Let's eat with our hands today. What do you say?'

'Is that something to ask about? Probably that's the problem with you famous people—everything about you makes headlines.'

'Don't chide me all the time. Tell me quickly how you like it.'

'A birthday treat like this after a long time. It's going to take me a while to take in the whole thing.'

'You still haven't started eating, so where does the question of taking in come from?'

'Did you add some salt to the rice?'

'Why, don't you add salt? Don't you like it? Sorry, I didn't know. Shall I quickly make some rice without salt?'

'Sorry, if you get so restless at a single word, then I can't tell you anything.'

'No, I thought you didn't like it.'

'Who said that? Did I say that even once?'

'You didn't, but looking at your eyes, I thought you didn't get the desired taste.'

'Outstanding! How much you can discern by just looking at my makeup-less eyes!'

'Please tell me; is it very bad?'

'It's very nice, really. It tastes completely different.'

'Different. Completely different? Great.'

'Stop talking and eat. Your rice is getting cold too.'

'Tinni, don't you wear anything else besides saris?'

'One has to; one can't wear a sari all the time.'

'Good joke. I like it. Rather, I appreciate it.'

'Intelligent!'

'Do you have any doubt?'

'Not at all. The food's simply great. It's true, true, true!'

'What does that mean?'

'It means for the next one month I won't like my own cooking anymore.'

'Okay, in that case, let's do one thing. I'll do a lot of shopping in the evening. After that, I'll cook the things I make well and leave them for you. You can take it out of the fridge and heat it up and have it.'

'I'll go mad; please don't say such things.'

'Go mad. Please, just once, for my sake.'

'You have no idea about the number of people who are crazy about you, and especially women; I'm just a boring teacher. It makes no difference whether you add me to that number or leave me out. But the way you're talking makes me wonder, if you have had a bet with someone regarding me.'

'What do you mean?'

'Meaning, say for instance, an experiment of entering into the sphere of a solitary person like me for a bit and seeing what happens by making me misbehave and take a misstep.'

'Perhaps this fear, terror, and suspicion of yours regarding any person and any situation is extremely normal. Believe me, Tinni, my thoughts regarding you are of a completely different nature.'

'Perhaps everybody thinks this way that I'm different, that my thoughts are of a different nature, but then somehow, everything remains just as painful. I can't take it anymore, you know. My rootlessness is far better. My self-made paradise and the hell of my own creation. The joy's mine; the suffering too is mine. There's no one else's participation, no obligations. Something that keeps returning, like morning, noon, and night.'

'If that's so, where do so many tears come from?'

'That's needed too, my conscious salvation.'

'Were you like this even when Rohini was here?'

'Exactly the same.'

'Sorry, I caused you anguish inadvertently. Believe me, it was not with any ill intention. If I had known that it would cause you more anguish, I wouldn't have done it at all.'

'Actually, I'm very stupid. I exhausted myself, you know, in the process of searching for what's good for me and leaving things out.'

'But you find and bring exceptional colors. It was Leena who first discovered this gift of yours.'

'Colors? Of what?'

'Of your saris, your curtains.'

'How did you see the color of my curtains? You haven't made a duplicate key to my room, have you?'

'Please, please, I've told you before as well. If I'm keen about you, that doesn't mean I'll go so far.'

'I still can't figure out how you found out the colour of the curtains.'

'Keep thinking, you'll know. The kitchen cloths too point to your sense of colour. The utensils…'

'A lot of those are Rohini's.'

'Do you think I didn't observe the changes after Rohini left?'

'Oh, you're a genius.'

'Do you accept that?'

'A hundred times.'

'Then give me a treat this evening, as it's your birthday.'

'What kind of treat would you like?'

'Don't leave it up to me. Do whatever you like.'

'You're right. If I leave it up to you, there's every possibility of me going bankrupt.'

'Hasn't that happened already, Tinni?'

'Don't try to make me agitated with everything you say. What's simply a joke for you may turn out to be terribly painful for me.'

'Always try to add a coat of the yellow of happiness or the colour red to the black of your anguish, and you'll see that you've created another beautiful colour. At first, you won't be able to think of a name for the color—you'll feel an uneasiness. But look at the color again and again, see it in different kinds of light, and all of a sudden, the depth of field changes, and an amazing sense begins operating in your mind, night and day, day and night…'

'But I don't want all that any more, and that's my *sadhana*.'

'Maybe I'm eager to know you because I do understand that.

But what about the treat? What's your plan?'

'Who told you that I'm planning?'

'I know.'

'Tell me which restaurants you like. I'll order dinner from one of them. You cooked and served me lunch; I'll serve you dinner.'

'Why won't you cook?'

'Didn't I tell you, I've been tired since morning. I just don't feel like working during the off days.'

'Finish your food, and you'll see that you feel a lot less tired. I'll make you a cocktail if you don't mind.'

'I do mind.'

'Are Baba, absolutely non-alcoholic. It'll only make you feel rejuvenated and taste great too. It's one of Suraj's recipes. You can learn a few. Some make you sleepy; some ease your aches; and some make you feel light-headed.'

'I must say you're extremely fortunate. You've got a good friend like Suraj.'

'You've found one too, but you don't want to accept that, or one could say that you're trying very hard to not accept that.'

'I cook the *posto* better than you.'

'You cook everything better than me.'

'Don't tease me. You've just had three or four things that I made; don't try to evaluate my Draupadi talent on that basis.'

'Draupadi talent—what's that?'

'Draupadi's culinary skills are mythical.'

'Really? I've never heard that before. Although my knowledge is only from Amar Chitra Katha and the television serials. I hardly even watched that.'

'And do you think I was Vyasa's friend?'

'No, that can't be. But you've become Dev's friend, even if it's just a bit.'

'Did you become my friend just because you did a lot of

work for me on my birthday and took a lot of care? Today, we had breakfast and lunch together and, for the first time, talked quite a lot. Only that part is true.'

'And tell me what's false?'

'Only the bit that's true belongs to the moment. The rest is nothing.'

'What remains, after all, Tinni? Suppose I'm sleeping and the entire aircraft that's carrying me sinks in the Pacific Ocean, then, only this day will remain true for you, as far as I am concerned. Don't think so much about the rest. After all, for the last three years, you've been trying very hard to cut the knot between truth and falsehood. Step outside your *lakshman rekha* once and just see that the world is one of tides.'

'Will you show me Anandi's picture?'

'I think you must've seen it when the room was being arranged.'

'I don't know. Rohini showed me some of your family photos. Shreya is very beautiful. Leena's also very sweet.'

'She's a crazy one. She's the most talented one of our generation, but her career is still not stable.'

'But I heard that she too is quite famous and popular. Although I didn't hear much about her from Rohini.'

'She's hardly met or talked to Rohini.'

'Tinni, do you mind, Ma… Ma's called, may I speak to her for a little while?'

'Of course, you needn't ask me. Take your time. I'll clear the table in the meantime.'

'You don't have to do that. I'll do it.'

'Not another word. Just talk to her.'

'Mom, today is Achira's birthday.'

'Achira—the lady with beauty and brains!'

'Yes, Rohini's friend.'

'Mine too.'

'Tinni, where are you? Mom wants to wish you.'

'Tinni?'

'Achira's pet name.'

'Just like her.'

'Tinni, Mom.'

'So nice of you! I don't know what to call you—Mrs. Dutta or Aunty? Birthday blessings from a Ma after three or four years. All because of Dev! Since this morning, he's been cooking so many things for me. And the *patrani machhi*, following your recipe, it was great!'

'Okay ladies, if you have anything more to talk about, I'll go to my room, or else leave it for another day.'

'Please come here. You won't have any problems here. I'm usually busy with college and study, so sharing the flat won't be a problem. I think Dev is waiting to talk to you. I'll call you later.'

'Thanks, I'll try to keep that in mind. Dev, Dev... where are you?'

'Come in, please, please...'

'You talk. I'll just finish something.'

'Come on, sit here. Let me tell Mother the tour details.'

'You talk, I'll be back just now.'

Chapter 7

I'm not doing the right thing. Why am I paying heed to Dev? I've gone by for a long time now on the basis of not needing anyone else in my life. So, what happened to that after all these days? I didn't feel any sense of inadequacy these last few years. After all, it was because a terrible sense of absence drove me to illness that I decided to live my life in a new way. Rohini—if Rohini hadn't brought me over at the time, I would've been dead and gone long ago. All by myself, I was discovering a new life—of surviving in a small world consisting only of myself.

'Have you started your soliloquy rehearsal again?'

'Why should it be a rehearsal? This is my place. And I want to remain stuck here. At least for the time being, I don't have any plans of getting out of here and entering any other sphere.'

'Tinni, how many things have you done in your life according to a plan? Matching it exactly to the design?'

'Don't call me Tinni all the time. It makes me uncomfortable.'

'Why? Did Shubhro call you Tinni all the time?'

'No, he never called me that.'

'So, did he call you by some name he invented?'

'No.'

'You're back to speaking in monosyllables. You really can. Will you teach it to me?'

'In some regards, people have to teach themselves.'

'Believe me, Tinni, no other profession but teaching would have suited you.'

'Meaning, I seem to be imparting wisdom, isn't it?'

'Not wisdom but a sermon.'

'*Phire jao! E topobon amar. Eke rokkha korar daayo amar.* Go back! This hermitage is mine. Protecting it is also my task.'

'Meaning, I'm trespassing; is that what you want to say?'

'I told you earlier, I don't want to say anything. I didn't want to before, and I don't want to in the future. If having me around is too problematic for you, I'll find a paying guest accommodation for myself. I only need two months.'

'Tinni, why do I seem inhuman to you? I have never been rude to you. And I never misbehaved with you in any way, so how can you talk to me like that?'

'Sorry. Sorry. I mean it, Dev.'

'I think I know you a lot.'

'I've spent my life in such a way that all my capabilities of discernment are confused. That's why I'm afraid. Afraid of becoming chaotic. Afraid of creating chaos. You won't understand, Dev. Your world of experience is entirely different.'

'Every person's world is different from another's, and that's normal. But it's by stitching together the bits of the differences that an entire life is created. That's why man goes around searching for his remaining bit.'

'Deeply philosophical talk. I think your fans would faint if they heard you say such things.'

'Why, who told you that all my fans are uneducated barbarians?'

'God! I didn't say that either. I was thinking about what would happen to those who see you as a glamour and fashion icon if they heard you say such things.'

'Brilliant! Tinni's concerned about my philosophical outlook.'

'No leg pulling, please.'

'Why do you always imagine that? After all, you're thinking about people all the time, but don't they have any other colors besides black and white?'

'They do. I've seen so many colors that I'm afraid of any further observation. I want my whole canvas to consist of just myself, Dev; that's why you see me muttering to myself and crying to myself— that's me communing with myself.'

'That's possible. Everyone has to do this to a greater or lesser degree. Or one could say, that's what we do. We all have to live with split personalities to some degree. But if you want to make that a practice, you might get into trouble at a certain point.'

'Hey, tell me quickly where I should order food from for dinner. Let me order it now.'

'The view from your balcony is really wide. Only a small curve of the sea is visible from my balcony. But from here—the whole of Mahalaxmi temple and on the other side, the beginning of Peddar Road.'

'There are so many people at Haji Ali today; see how the waves are surging.'

'You know, all of them will shut their eyes and sit on their knees… like this… at the dargah, and offer a prayer for your birthday. They'll lay a chadar lovingly over the tomb. They'll hold out their hands in prayer, seeking blessings for you. Put your hands over your eyes and see that there's no more darkness today—all is light. That light is split into seven colors. Let's go and buy saris of all the colors; come, let's go.'

'Birthdays have a fabulous aura when you're a child. Preparations begin so many days ahead. New clothes. Ma's plans for the food to be prepared. Thinking about who to invite. Even a special puja for the birthday.'

'Come, let's go and perform a puja today. Shall we go to Mahalaxmi temple?'

'With you?'

'Why? Can't I go?'

'Of course you can go. Maybe you go to temples. I don't know. But don't you get mobbed in all these public places?'

'Oh, there are arrangements for all that. Would you like to go?'

'No.'

'Why not?

'I don't go to any temples anymore.'

'You don't go anymore? Meaning, you did go at one time?'

'Yes. I used to go. I don't go now. And I don't have any urge to go today either.'

'Alright, go when you feel like. How windy it is! It's as if the waves want to come and touch your feet.'

'I haven't wet my feet in the sea for over a year. Without Rohini here, all my urges seem to have turned hollow. I just walk along the sea's edge. I don't go near the water.'

'Me neither. I go for shoots, but that's just a part of the unit's job, a part of the production. I'm just a character in that.'

'I'll invite Leena one day when you're back.'

'Invite me when I'm back. You can invite Leena in the meantime. But keep some time in hand. There'll be so much talk that you'll need time to get rid of your headache.'

'I can see that today.'

'Meaning, do you want to say that you have a headache from talking to me?'

'Not yet, but it's time now. It's been a long time since I talked to or listened to someone for so long.'

'It feels like you're attending some refresher course, doesn't it?'

'It does.'

'What about the facilitator's honorarium?'

'Is that still due?'

'Why? When did you ever pay me anything?'

'I've been jabbering away since morning, listening to you. I've gone way beyond my normal routine. Isn't that enough?'

'You're simply great.'

'So I am. What do you want to eat? Indian or Chinese or Italian? Or something else? I don't really know what's available where.'

'Your birthday lunch was at home; let's go out for dinner.'

'For you, going out means some five-star restaurant. But won't it be a bit difficult for me to afford that?'

'Do you want to take a loan from me?'

'No. Isn't it stretching things too far to take a loan from you to give you a treat?'

'So, you stretch things a bit to make the birthday memorable.'

'The memorable birthday will be observed after I die, by those who remain.'

'Your students are great fans of yours, aren't they?'

'They're not what a "fan" is commonly understood to mean, but yes, I realize some of them like me.'

'Like Leena.'

'The students like me for my style of teaching, that's all.'

'And your colleagues?'

'Most of my colleagues think I'm mad or some kind of inhumane creature. So, they hardly pay any attention to me.'

'Actually, most people are afraid of you because you wear a feelings-proof jacket. Have you made any friends in college all these days?'

'No. I have no need for friends.'

'May I smoke a cigarette? I haven't had one in a long while.'

'I don't think there's any need to take my permission.'

'Your name, I mean, the name *Achira* is very appropriate.'

'Say what you want to clearly; don't talk in riddles.'

'Achira, meaning lightning. A sudden flash of light, but before you know it, the sense you're left with is not just of light but darkness too; a complex kind of sense seizes you.'

'My Ma also used to say that I had a difficult kind of nature.'

'Why did she say that?'

'Maybe because I hardly cried. I used to be very quiet when I was young—I mean, when I was in school.'

'And you changed once you entered college?'

'I didn't change completely. But when I liked the environment and the people, I began to talk. You could say I was always of a submissive nature. I changed bit by bit without even being aware of it.'

'Did you fall in love before meeting Shubhro?'

'It's my first love that's still with me.'

'Please say it simply. I'll be stumped if you talk so cerebrally.'

'When I was in the sixth standard, I became acquainted with a poet.'

'Cinematic!'

'I became acquainted with his poetry. We had to read that in class. I didn't have the opportunity to meet the poet. Because I was born too late, the poet left this strange world in outrage. But like the body armor and earrings that Karna was born with, I was born in this very world with all the feelings of separation from my poet.'

'You lost me completely, Tinni. Seriously.'

'Can I ask you for something?'

'Ask me?'

'Yes, ask you.'

'Tell me, what do you want?'

'Will you give me a cigarette?'

'Oh, I thought you might demand a birthday gift, like when you were small. Of course, I don't know whether you would actually ask. I used to demand: a wooden cricket bat, a full-size football, a tennis racquet, clothes that I fancied, a camera, a music system, my own TV, a motorbike… I asked for all that on various birthdays, sometimes from my Baba and sometimes from my Ma.'

'I too used to ask for so many things as a child: books with colored pictures, a glass flower vase, a long frock with flower prints, Rajasthani jootis, anklets, hair clips, a harmonium, a tanpura, notebooks for writing, an engraved jewelry box, a magic box to keep bangles, a Kashmiri powder container made of papier-mache, a dokra candle stand, so many things… I can't even remember all of them now.'

'Childhood is precious, isn't it?'

'Maybe not for everyone. For instance, it's great in a certain way for you, and in another way for me. But again, many people have difficult childhoods. Not just about having or not having money, a lot depends on whether one's parents get along or don't get along.'

'Who do you remember most on your birthday? Your Ma? Baba?'

'No one at all.'

'That can't be true.'

'Really, I don't remember anyone very much now. I think my roots have come loose. Now, I think no one was ever mine. That I wasn't anyone's either.'

'Don't talk like the verses from the Gita. The you that is you keeps talking to another you…'

'You haven't given me a cigarette yet.'

'Sorry, I'm giving it to you…'

'My stock's finished. I forgot about it.'

'It's okay. I have plenty. How many do you want?'

'I don't have any fixed number per day. It goes up and down, depending on my urge. Some days it is a single one, and sometimes it may even be ten or twelve. It depends entirely on my mood.'

'That means this isn't really an addiction.'

'Of course, it's an addiction! Whatever's determined by my wishes is simply an addiction!'

'No, it's your luxury.'

'I can't agree that my smoking is a luxury.'

'Whether you agree or not is your business. Can I also smoke one with you?'

'Why should I come in the way of what you want to do?'

' Look at the sky, instead of arguing with me. So many shades of colors. Just see how many shades there are even of red. Look at that corner; it's as if the colour of your sari's border comes from there.'

'There were three *krishnachura* trees in our house in Balurghat. From my window, it looked as if the red flowers had lit up the sky. There were mud roads, and once it rained, the water flooding the road was all red. Once I grew up, one by one, all the colors gradually left me. I think I began looking inward, after I realized that.'

'Did you find it?'

'What?'

'Colors. The childhood magic of the *krishnachura* and earth that you lost.'

'I thought I had found it many times. But soon after, I realized it wasn't exactly that. What I'd find was either a lighter shade than that or a bit deeper.'

'But even in the difference between what we set out to find and what we eventually find, we get something, which too forms us. Like today, what you got or are getting instead of sleeping is definitely not worthless, don't you think?

'What it is for me, I can't tell you right now; actually, I can't explain it to you. And as for myself, I don't want to know about it.'

'Don't! Come, let's go and buy glass bangles.

'I've buried that age and those urges long ago.'

'Do you see the small plant that's grown on that? The plant doesn't have a name. But lots and lots of yellow flowers bloom in clusters on it.'

'You would have made quite a name for yourself even if you had become a poet.'

'Who told you that I'm not a poet? Not just the feelings of separation like your poet, I have a sense of heartening hope too.'

'I have another poet as well. But he is just too famous. My love affair with him began when I was a bit older.'

'Was the first poet Tagore?'

'No, he was the second. I got the sense of love from him.'

'And the first love?'

'I can't tell you the name now.'

'Why not? There's no chance of a scandal or gossip in this regard, so why can't you reveal the name?'

'It's public figures like you who get involved in scandals. The big-name media sells gossip and earns millions of rupees. The matter of the relationship between my poet and me is entirely secret. The name is the seed-mantra there. It can't be uttered at any odd time or to anyone else.'

'I realize I haven't yet reached that station.'

'That requires *sadhana*.'

'I'm willing to do that. Tell me, what's the way to the *sadhana*?'

'I don't think there's any particular way. One doesn't even know in advance when and how it hits the right note.'

'That means one has to wait, isn't it?'

'One of our teachers used to say that there must be clouds of yearning, only then can it rain.'

'Come, Tinni, let's go for a short drive. I feel like being outdoors in this wonderful weather. Like to go?'

'Not today.'

'Then tell me when you'll have the time. I'll wait with clouds of yearning.'

'We should call Rohini, you know.'

'How did Rohini suddenly come into the picture?'

'I have so much now that I got from Rohini that she's with me all the time. Unless Rohini arrived in Kolkata that fateful day, no one would have even found me. Maybe once the body decomposed and stank, it would be known that I had died.'

'Wasn't Shubro in Kolkata then?'

'I don't think so.'

'And your parents?'

'They were in the house in Haldia.'

'Had you left Kolkata long before that?'

'No. It must have been about three months.'

'Rohini told me a little bit.'

'Did you want to know?'

'A little bit. She told me how I should conduct myself with you—she wanted to explain that to me. She said I shouldn't make things difficult for you or disturb you in any way. Things like that.'

'Rohini is like a goddess to me. The way she saved me single-handedly, I'm amazed every time I think about it. She fought all the odds entirely by herself, which was unknown to me. Samir supported her a lot. Bringing me over to Bombay, and then my treatment, getting me to start reading again, finding me a job— everything's because of her.'

'Because of her I could get so close to a person like you. Feels nice to think about that.'

'Is the fact that I'm alone such a big deal for you?'

'No. Not at all.'

'Then what is it?'

'Your entire presence draws me powerfully. Perhaps because our outward lives are so different, an initial feeling of astonishment was created. There was something else that made me think a lot, and I still think about it. You can completely ignore everything around you.'

'A terribly nose-in-the-air type…'

'Not exactly nose-in-the-air, you move about as if you're some kind of celestial body. Here, but not here. But I always feel your presence very strongly.'

'One spring, setting afloat a *polash* flower in the university lake, a pair of entranced eyes said, "I gave all of myself to the *polash* flower; my time will touch through the water."'

'Where was Shubhro then?'

'What do you mean *where*?'

'Were you married then?'

'No. I wasn't married then.'

'Let me show you Anandi's picture. Please come to my room.'

'Let's go. By the way, shall I change the living room a bit?'

'You're asking me?'

'Do you think I'm asking the walls?'

'You may well do that, you know; perhaps they're closer to you. I've suddenly landed from some faraway planet.'

'Why should that be? You have a fifty percent right to the living room. And so, if anything's to be changed, your opinion and consent are required.'

'What do I have to do to give my opinion and consent?'

'You don't have to do anything for now. Let me think about it some more; I'll let you know later. And yes, another thing: if it costs too much, I'll ask you to share the amount.'

'You plan it out and let me know. I can leave a couple of signed checks, you know. Of course, that's if you don't mind.'

'Just inform Suraj. And after all, you'll be back in a month. It'll take me some time to get the work done. Let me think some more about what to get done.'

'Think about the lighting too, whether something can be changed. Let me know if you have any other suggestions. But of course, you'll be very busy as always; you won't have time to think about such things.'

'You take care of all that. Call me and let me know, or email me. Is this Anandi?'

'Yes!'

'Wow! Very beautiful!

'There used to be a lot of talk about her in college.'

'I'm sure there was a lot of talk about you as well?'

'A little bit.'

'That means you were a hotly discussed couple in college.'

'How can I say whether it was hotly discussed? But yeah, we were talkcd about.'

'Did everyone know about your affair?'

'Yes. From the principal to the watchman. Everyone.'

'Do you know the person Anandi married?'

'No.'

'So, he's not from your college or your circle of acquaintances?'

'No. He's from Mangalore.'

'Have you met Anandi's husband?'

'No.'

'Why not? Didn't you ever want to?'

'Not at all. Do you ever want to know how Shubhro is now?'

'No. Never. But you don't have any bitter memories of Anandi. It was you who said that you don't have any complaints regarding Anandi.'

'Yes, I don't have any. But I have no interest at all as far as Anandi's husband is concerned.'

'See how it suddenly turned dark. Only a couple of lights far away.'

'Why does light behave in this way, Tinni? A faraway light draws you near, but why does the nearby light keep pushing you afar?'

'The nearby light is useful for us, so maybe there's nothing as enchanting about that. But with the faraway light, it's the distance that prompts imagination. For me, even the nearby light often seems entrancing, especially if the light is of a soft, yellow kind. White light doesn't attract me. Maybe that's because that light is far too necessary.'

'Did you do the lighting scheme in your room?'

'It's not a scheme or anything. Didn't I tell you I liked soft yellow light? So, I've put some lights like that in the room.'

'Will you let your yellow light shower on me?'

'Say the yellow light of my room. Anandi is quite tall too, isn't she?'

'Five-seven-and-a-half.'

'Is she in Toronto now? You can look her up this time.'

'No. I've no urge to do that.'

'Right. If you have no interest, it's best not to do it.'

'Here, see my first portfolio.'

'You looked quite different.'

'Really? I was young. It's from seven or eight years ago; that's quite long ago.'

'That's right. But my battle's gone on even longer.

'What battle, Tinni? In the name of this splendid evening, will you tell me?'

'If I ever think it's necessary to tell someone other than myself, I'll think of you first.'

'Did you talk to Shubhro too in the same way?'

'I think with Shubhro, it was I who did most of the talking.

He never paid any attention. Of course, I was very slow to realize the truth.'

'Look at this photo of mine; I got an entry to the Gladrags Contest by sending this. Did you ever keep track of such things?'

'I didn't really keep track as such, but it's not like I knew nothing. I had seen your images as a model.'

'Have you seen any movies of mine?'

'Rohini had taken me along once.'

'Did you enjoy the movie?'

'I wasn't exactly in a condition to enjoy anything. She said I could stay in this flat. So, she was kind of training me.'

'Rohini told me never to transgress your *lakshman rekha* even by mistake.'

'And yet you intentionally…'

'Yes, intentionally, but not to trouble you. The wish to do so grew bit by bit. I even disagreed with myself sometimes. But then it occurred to me that this wasn't right. After all, you're not a tiger or a bear.'

'But she's crazy! She might scratch and bite you!'

'I've observed your crazy ways for quite some time. Your craziness is not action-oriented, and it was only once that was confirmed…'

'That you did what?'

'That I decided to talk to you. I talked to Rohini too during this time.'

'Did Rohini tell you to take interest in me?'

'Absolutely not. She told me time and again that I must never hurt you in any way.'

'I don't know. I don't feel like arguing any more today. My self-preparation isn't complete yet.'

'That's best. Once it's complete, then there'll be nothing left to argue about!'

'Raju and I had arranged your wardrobe. Did you find everything that you wanted when required?'

'I haven't used it very much. I'll ask you if necessary. You can tell me. I think the phone is ringing in your room.'

'Can you hear it from here? I didn't hear it.'

'I observe everything about you closely; do you understand Tinni?'

'While I'm completely indifferent to you, is that what you want to say?'

'Whether I want to say it or not is immaterial. It's the truth.'

'The world of my needs is so small that it's quite unusual for a big-time person like you to enter it.'

'Not a big-time person. Say it's some man with a different life than yours.'

'Exactly. Besides, I don't really need anything anymore from a man or anyone for that matter. That's why I never felt the urge to make any friends in college either.'

'But you had to listen to me blabbering all day on your birthday; that wasn't too bad, was it?'

'It wasn't bad, but I wouldn't have felt bad in any way even if this hadn't happened. There wouldn't have been any regret. I might have slept a lot and sat down to do some more writing. My birthday doesn't have any special significance for me anymore. Maybe it's the same for everyone. It's only the marketplace that cares. It's all just an exaggeration of product marketing.'

'But I didn't do anything like that. And yet you're scolding me.'

'Why should I scold you? I'm only trying to make my position clear to myself.'

'You didn't pick up the phone. It might be something important.'

'Importance has to be mutual. I don't think there's anyone who would have anything important to communicate to me.'

'It could also be from home.'

'Home meaning?'

'Your Ma and Baba.'

'They don't know my whereabouts. They didn't try to find out either.'

'You could have informed them that you're well; you could have simply let them know that you're alright.'

'Maybe they'd have been stressed knowing I'm still around. They'd feel ill at ease; that's why I didn't inform them. And I have no plans to do so either.'

'Do you know about them—I mean, how they are getting on?'

'I know, but again I don't know as well.'

'Meaning?'

'Rohini informs me from time to time. I never tried to find out what the source of her information was over the last three years. I didn't stop her from telling me either, so that's it.'

'As soon as it gets dark, the lights on Peddar Road appear to be standing like solitary sentinels. Suraj is very happy that I live in this location. Most of the people in my work sphere like the stretch from Bandra to the western suburbs.'

'Don't you have any plans of building your own house?'

'It's not like I have no plans at all, but I think I'm a bit superstitious because of my career graph since I moved into this flat. It's not easy to predict whether one will have work or not.'

'Do you mean to say this flat has been lucky for you?'

'You could say that.'

'Then why don't you do something—buy this flat for yourself. Rohini is prepared to sell it if she finds a proper buyer. And she likes you a lot. She's almost family to you all. She'll be happy if you buy this flat.'

'Maybe. But…'

'But what? I'm here for now—is that a problem?'

'Not the least bit. Don't talk like that.'

'Given your profile now, it'll really be problematic for you to share a flat with someone. I know about these things quite well. I can give you my word that there'll be no trouble from my side.'

'Tinni, I'm really sorry. If I ever do anything that causes you anguish, please forgive me.'

'I only need time to find a paying guest accommodation, say a month. I haven't forgotten what you did for me during my difficult time, Dev. So, there won't be any problem from my side.'

'Listen, first of all, I don't have any plans to buy this flat. And if I do buy it, that will only happen if you continue to stay here, in the same way as you are now.' 'That's not possible.' 'Why's it not possible? Because Rohini is your friend, while I'm nobody?'

'You need a large, and if possible, even larger flat or house now. The dimensions of an ordinary person's needs and those of people like you are quite different. That's true, and there's no way you can deny that.'

'This is why Suraj calls you "Master-ji."'

'Really? Our watchman and liftman also call me Master-ji. The first day Raju and his men came looking for your flat, the watchman told them to go to Master-ji's flat. He asked me later why you were living at my place. Why you didn't have a place of your own, and so on.'

'Great! I thought Suraj called you Master-ji because he's scared of you and wants to maintain a distance.'

'We used to call the tailor, Master-ji.'

'We did the same too.'

'If we got the picture of our adulthood bit by bit during our childhood, then one would have suffered much less, isn't it?'

'That's true. Of course, the preparation time turns out to be useful in some way or the other… See, here's my childhood album. Most of the pictures were taken by Baba. See how I was posing even then! Please don't laugh; I'll feel terribly ashamed.'

'Still ashamed?'

'Why? Do you think I'm absolutely shameless?'

'When did I say that? Listen, we haven't ordered dinner yet.'

'So, we can't do anything. No dinner tonight.'

'Finish your packing. Let me see what can be ordered.'

'Sit here quietly and look at the pictures. Let me check to see if I've forgotten anything.'

'You do that carefully. I'll be in my room.'

'Yes, do that. I'll freshen up and come to your room.'

'Your wishes keep spreading their wings.'

'They've been doing that for a long time. It took you time to realize that because you don't pay any attention.'

'I don't have any desire to know.'

'Are wishes like some concrete platform that they don't change?'

'When one holds one's wishes tightly within one's fist, their form changes. They shrink and become so small that whatever's left is not for sharing with anyone else. Actually, virtually nothing remains when you open your fist, there are only the lines on the palm which never leave you. Body-armor or amulets are futile against fate.'

'You lost me again. You could also take a shower. I'll join you in five minutes.'

Chapter 8

Let's look at the adverse side now. There are a few more hours left for the thing that began today to come to an end. That's what it is. How would it be if I changed my residence even before he returns? But why am I thinking like this? Why do I have to escape? Why am I getting afraid like this about myself once again? I don't like it. Why didn't Rohini forbid Dev when he inquired about talking to me? Why did she tell Dev about my birthday? But I don't feel like talking about these things with Rohini. Why am I doing what I don't want to do? Why am I talking about dinner? How can I get out of it? I can't think of anything. There's the doorbell. Someone's come. Must be Dev's guest. I'll be spared. If it's one of his friends, I'll be relieved from talking anymore today. I have talked a lot in the last few hours. But if I shut the door and switch off the light, I can convey to Dev, for now, that I'm not willing to talk any more. No, that would be extremely childish. Besides, considering whatever he's done for me since morning, as a flat mate, I ought to treat him to dinner. But why am I changing again? No, I've been wearing this sari since noon. It's well past the time I would have changed according to my usual routine. What can I wear? Maroon or mulberry? Or shall I wear the muga-silk sari? Have I gone mad? Why am I thinking so much? But why can't I think? It's my birthday today. Even when I used to go out with Rohini, I used to open the wardrobe and think about what to wear. Even when I go to college, I think every day about what sari to wear. After all, this is something I've done since childhood. Let me wear the maroon sari. I haven't worn it in a long time. After all, I'm not changing because of what Dev will think or say. I'm only doing what I like to do and like to wear. But why does the thought of altering myself because of Dev's presence keep occurring to me? Why do I feel so uncomfortable? Why am I even giving it so much importance? I need to change my strategy once I cordially complete what began today.

'Hi Tinni, may I come in?'

'Sorry, Dev. I need another five minutes, please.'

'Alright, I'm lighting a cigarette on your balcony. Don't be late. What on earth were you doing all this while?'

'I'll tell you when I come out.'

'Why don't you tell me from inside? I can hear you. I'm used to secretly listening to your singing.'

'I think I ought to fix a door in the passage now.'

'Instead of rewarding me for revealing the truth, you're thinking of how to punish me.'

'I wonder how you can go on jabbering like this.'

'And are you short of things to say? You were muttering again a little while ago.'

'I hope you haven't installed some device in your room that can penetrate through walls and hear everything I say.'

'If only there were something like that.'

'I warn you.'

'I'm also warning you; no more delay. I've got to come inside to see what you're up to.'

'Come in.'

'Are you sure?'

'Don't play the fool. Come in.'

'Wow! Fabulous color.'

'Of what?'

'The walls.'

'Your room too has the same shade.'

'But in your room, it looks more soothing.'

'You're talking like a child.'

'Why's that?'

'Liking others' things better than one's own.'

'Are all these books yours?'

'No, your uncle's!'

'Did you buy this music system recently?'

'No. It's Rohini's.'

'There's some problem in my music system. Someone was supposed to come and take a look at it this week. But no one came.'

'I was there when Raju and others were working in your room.'

'It was working fine just a few days back. There was some problem yesterday. I've told Suraj. Will you do me a favor?'

'Tell me.'

'No, let it be.'

'Why?

'I don't think I should bother you.'

'Hey, you've come into my room, and you're still standing here. Of course, I don't have a lavish seating arrangement like you have in your room. I don't need that either. I like this kind of seating scheme.'

'It's the first time I'm entering your room. I've known you for over two years. Lived next to you. But you allowed me in for the first time today.'

'The need didn't arise, and that's why you didn't enter. Really, you could have entered if you needed to, like Leena did. Suppose you were at home, and I had fainted in my room, and you discovered that somehow, then obviously you would have come into my room without waiting for my invitation or permission.'

'But I had invited you into my room on the very first day we met. You said something or the other and evaded that.'

'Really? I can't exactly remember.'

'Oh, you do remember, alright! If we exclude today, you could count the number of sentences we exchanged in a single hand.'

'Sit down. Shall I put on some music?'

'You'll play it for me?'

'The music system will play it.'

'Why don't you sing?'

'I just don't feel comfortable sitting in front of someone and singing.'

'In that case, I'll go to the balcony, and you can sit in the room and sing. Or go to the balcony and sit in your favorite posture and sing, and I'll sit in your room and hear you.'

'Tell me quickly now, what do you want to eat? I've been asking you that since the afternoon.'

'I want to eat a slice of black forest gateau now; after that, a piece of chocolate pie, a scoop of tender coconut ice cream, and also something else I was dying to have… I can't remember that now. I'll tell you as soon as I remember.'

'Tell me all the places I should call to get these. Give me the numbers. I'll order it for you.'

'Sing a song, and you'll see everything arriving before you.'

'I got it; that's why the doorbell rang sometime back.'

'Yes, when you were in your solitary soliloquy. By the way, the color of your sari is fabulous.'

'You've used hyperbolic adjectives all day. Do say something else that's believable—that can be relied upon.'

'If I knew you'd believe it, the sea would turn bluer. Will you do something, Tinni?'

'What?'

'Why don't you go to the kitchen and bring down the box?'

'You have a terrible thrashing in your fate'.

'Only in my fate?'

'Ha, ha, cheesy, filmy!'

'What's to be done? It's my livelihood for survival! Hey Tinni, the film of mine that you watched with Rohini, how did you like that?'

'I won't be able to say very much about it. Please, don't examine me. I'll fail badly.'

'Why? Did you sleep all the while you were in the movie theater?'

'No, but I wasn't in the right frame of mind. I wasn't interested in anything at all.'

'Did you see that I was in the film?'

'Yes, that's all I saw. I would have to live with this screen-man a few days later, sharing a kitchen and other common facilities. There were various thoughts weighing on my mind.'

'And after that, when I actually moved in, what did you think?'

'I used to feel uncomfortable at first. After that, since you were hardly here, most of my anxieties passed gradually.'

'And now?'

'I'm worried a lot.'

'Why?'

'About whether I would start looking for people to talk to once again.'

'Don't look for people. After all, Dev's here.'

'No. There's no one. There shouldn't be anyone. Only Achira, *advitiya*.'

'*Advitiya*. But not alone. Lightning has clouds; it has the sun and howling wind; it has disheveled *anchals*; it has the melody of falling rain.'

'Who was more poetic? Anandi or Sumedha?'

'Sumedha was terribly immature compared to Anandi. Anandi was extremely balanced. She's a genius.'

'Shounak used to write very well.'

'He liked you very much.'

'But he never told me that.'

'What didn't he tell you?'

'About whether he liked or disliked me.'

'You belonged to the great lady. Everyone knew about the "arranged affair" with the great lady's son.'

'When did Shounak tell you all this?'

'Before I moved in, I was trying to find out whatever I could about you. Rohini gave me that reference when she first spoke about you to me. And then, while talking to Shounak, I realized we had talked about you several times earlier.'

'What rubbish!'

'It's true. It's a small world, don't you think?'

'Not just small, but completely flat as well.'

'You're a genius' genius!'

'Once Shounak and I evaded all our friends and went to see a film, did he tell you that?'

'No, he didn't tell me.'

'I used to stay in the hostel at that time. I had come to Kolkata just a few days before that.'

'Meaning, that lady had not yet discovered you.'

'The discovery was mutual.'

'You thought that if you could live under the shadow of such a person, you'd have no more worries in life.'

'It's not that I thought that way initially. But I had just begun my academic journey, and at that time, she became my guide at every step. She was impossibly erudite and brilliant. You could say I was completely mesmerized.'

'You thought a place in paradise has been carved out for you.'

'Maybe I thought so. Forget it; is this your subject for the evening? In that case, I want to be excused.'

'What should the subjects be, so that you never ask to be excused?'

'Shall I sing a song?'

'I've been asking you to sing all this while, but you don't bother about a listener like me.'

'I, myself, am the listener to my songs, as is the surging sea breeze. I don't wait for anyone else. I hope I could make you understand what I'm trying to say.'

'Please, no more harsh words today.'

'Sorry, that's the kind of person I am. Not at all balanced like Anandi.'

'How did the question of comparison with Anandi come up?'

'It's not a comparison… don't I know that? I think I'm really going mad. I've lost my sense of how I should talk to people. I'm really sorry. Please don't mind. I don't know why my past doesn't leave me. It's been so long. I've come a long way, but the shackles remain.'

'The more you hold on to the thought of the shackles in order to survive, the stronger they become.'

'I think I had started loving the shackles themselves, like a blind person.'

'Open your eyes now, Tinni. Just look; far away, somewhere on that sea, is another place that's waiting for you.'

'A dream. I don't have the courage anymore; my sea is full of salty water.'

'But this water's sweet, isn't it? Can I have some?'

'Sorry, I haven't even offered you some water.'

'I'd like some, please. But will you only offer me water?'

'What would you like to have? Wait, there's an indigenous drink I really like; I'll make it for you.'

'Is the recipe yours?'

'It's just something I improvised.'

'What kind of lemon is this?'

'It's called *gondhoraj*.'

'Fantastic. You added rock salt, didn't you? Won't you add anything sweet?'

'I'll do that. Instead of jabbering away, just sit down quietly.'

'What else will you offer me if I sit down quietly?'

'That ice cream and whatever else you got.'

'Your favorite "Naturals" ice cream; you must have it first. The drink's exceptional. If I ever start a restaurant, I'll keep you as an adviser.'

'How could you think that I would work for you?'

'What if the salary is a six-figure one, would you still not do it?'

'No. I don't believe I can do anything right now other than teach.'

'My dear, that's also teaching. You'll advise me, so that means you're my teacher.'

'Again, the private property.'

'It's difficult to match you with reason.'

'As difficult as me.'

'But you're easy-difficult.'

'Let me show you a hilarious picture; it's from Rohini's collection.'

'She has still kept all these pictures carefully. Rohini's elder sister was a common friend of Shreya and me.'

'I've heard some stories, Rohini told me.'

'While giving you my resume?

'Yes.'

'Where shall we cut the cake, Tinni?'

'No cake-cutting or anything, please.'

'That means the two of us will grab it with our hands like children and eat it.'

'I've never eaten a cake in that way. I never had any great love for sweet things.'

'But smearing a birthday cake on the face is more fun than eating it.'

'There was no cake-cutting in my childhood. Ma used to make payesh.'

'But *payesh* is also sweet.'

'That's why I used to have just a spoonful as a ritual.'

'I don't know how to prepare *payesh*. So let the ritual be completed with the cake this birthday. I give you my word; I'll learn to make *payesh* before next year.'

'You don't have to give me any words.'

'Why are you always so skeptical? Relax!'

'If my life had been smooth sailing like yours, perhaps I could have relaxed.'

'Do you think it's only those famous, high-profile magazines that know what my life's like? Do you know what living on the edge means? You can do a few things like earn your income in the way you like, and spend your time in an amazing world of your own creation. I don't think there are too many intruders like me in your life. But think about me, or those like me. Everything's public. Everything's fabricated.'

'That too is according to your wishes.'

'Yes, I agree, but one doesn't realize when wishes and compulsion, which are two different things, become one.'

'Do all these professional hazards make you unhappy?'

'Won't they? Am I a machine? That has no feelings?'

'Shall we try to heal the machine's anguish for now with a bite of black forest?'

'Of course, bring the candles!'

'Good God!'

'Just listen to whatever I say like a good girl. Ma used to say that when I was small, you remember that, don't you?'

'How would I know what your Ma used to tell you?'

'Arey, not just my Ma, everyone's Ma says, "Don't do anything on your birthday to make me scold you. Be good the whole day. Listen to everything I say." Now, Tinni, be a good girl and go and bring one of those fragrant candles. I'll sing the birthday jingle all by myself.'

'How did you find out about the candles?'

'It'll be time for my flight if I keep answering these questions of yours. Do you want to have the cake and the other things all by yourself? Or are you planning to have a birthday party tomorrow with all your students?'

'So, was that your homework, and were those your observations?'

'Poor. Let it be. If the birthday girl is still not ready to cut the cake, then you are entirely responsible for what happens next.'

'Are you threatening me?'

'No. I'm scared.'

'Smart.'

'Any doubts?'

'Where's your cake?'

'Come to the living room. How about bringing it to your room? Or rather, let's cut the cake in the living room and celebrate on the balcony. Our very special party.'

'Let's take the cake there.'

'Didn't I tell you? Don't be disobedient. Get up, or else I'll have to carry you.'

'I miss Rohini terribly.'

'You'll miss lots of people. You can do all that after cutting the cake. I'm very hungry too, and I'm sure my delightful decoration has gone to the dogs by now.'

'What do you mean by decoration? I don't want any of that.'

'What do you mean you "don't want"? Shut your eyes. Have you ever woken up in the middle of the night and walked to the kitchen or living room?'

'No.'

'Alright. Don't worry. Just hold my hand, and make sure your eyes are shut tight. No cheating.'

'I'm coming… let's go.'

'Don't say that with such reluctance. Think of your host and be a bit happy.'

'I can only think about myself and be happy. The days of being happy thinking about someone else are long gone. I know you won't like to hear that, but that's what I'm like.'

'If you say another word…'

'What will you do?'

'I'll call the police.'

'The complaint?'

'The reason for my heart attack. If only I could sing like Bryan Adams, "Everything I do…"'

'I find such things very painful. You won't understand. You'll think I'm being stubborn.'

'No more talk. Not another word. Happy Birthday to you!'

'Why have you kept everything in darkness?'

'Because everything will come alight.'

'Don't try to be poetic.'

'May I kiss you?'

'Just shut up.'

'Arey, just a birthday kiss. I'll just touch my lips to your shut eyelids. And then there'll be magic. All the lights will come on. From head to toe.'

'Please keep quiet.'

'Open your mouth! I'll feed you cake. Like your Ma.'

'I just don't know.'

'You just don't know what to do with me… Isn't that what you wanted to say?'

'The cake is marvelous.'

'That's not because of where it's come from. It's because of me. Because of my wishes. Because of my enchantment. Because of my amazement.'

'Thanks.'

'Just "thanks"? I deserve at least a big hug.'

'You deserve a lot more. But I'm not the right person. There's only one thing I'd like to say—be well.'

'That's what I want to say too, Tinni—be well. Wear that smile in your eyes.'

'I'm really doing well. And that is largely because of Rohini. There's also your contribution to that. But you could say my solitude is my *tapasya*. That's how I can advance bit by bit…'

'Feed me cake first. Arey Baba, that's the rule. If you follow the birthday rule, your wish will be fulfilled.'

'You're simply impossible…'

'The cake's really nice. I'm having it after a long time. I think it tastes even better than the last time.'

'You like it more because you're having it on my birthday.'

'It tastes even better because you fed it to me.'

'Come, let's go and sit on the balcony.'

'I'll take the things there one by one, alright?'

'What time will you leave?'

'Are you sad? Shall I cancel the trip?'

'You talk such rubbish.'

'Are you calculating—how much longer do you have to suffer my oppression?'

'Is everything just black or white, good or bad, Dev?'

'God! But the black-and-white era ended long ago…'

'You're always ready with words, aren't you?'

'Words are my profession—diction, gesture—such expertise is very useful; you know that quite well. You could say I'm just trying to impress you a bit with all that.'

'You're trying to impress me? Why? I'm one of the most unwanted people in the world. Your fame, prestige, etcetera are the stuff of lots of people's dreams, urges, and envy. But I'm simply a non-entity in comparison.'

'Theory, theory, more theory…'

'Where's the theory? It's deep application.'

'Tinni, does it ever occur to you that what happened to you was not normal and that your life should have been different?

'Maybe.'

'Don't say maybe. That won't be true, even to yourself. And that's why your personal truth seems to you to be a universal truth. You just want to hold on to that with all your life.'

'It's nice to see the breadth of your thinking. But your understanding doesn't match who I am. It's normal that it doesn't match. But I think my view is perhaps different.'

'Explain to me where I'm going wrong.'

'It's not something that can be put into a few words.'

'Then explain it to me at length.'

'It's not yet time for that.'

'How was that decided?'

'It concerns me, so I ought to know the urge. If I ever think it's appropriate, I'll surely tell you.'

'I hope you'll remember that.'

'My memory is not like camphor. That's why I have a knotty problem.'

'May I come and sit beside you?'

'You're already sitting near me.'

'I didn't say near… beside?'

'I think sitting facing each other is the best way to say or hear something. After all, you're an expert on that too; I don't need to explain that to you.'

'Shall we have the chocolate pie now?'

'I can't eat anything more now. You go ahead.'

'We can share one. I too have to think of the calories.'

'In that case, I won't eat any more now. Pack it in a box and take it along. Eat it later.'

'Rubbish! This was to sit and have with you. If we can't have it today, then I'll have it when I return after a month. Keep it for me. Don't have it all by yourself!'

'Can you imagine what it will be like after a month in the fridge? It'll become stiff like jaggery *batasha*.'

'What's *batasha*?'

'It's a kind of special, dry sweet made out of sugar or jaggery.'

'Then it's better if I have one now; I'll worry about the consequences later.'

'You'll have to work out a lot again to burn those calories.'

'What do you do?'

'What do you mean, "what do I do"?'

'For fitness?'

'What on earth should I do? Ordinary people like me don't have to do all that.'

'Rubbish, you don't know anything at all. Do you think all the gyms and fitness equipment in the world are for those in the show business?'

'I don't know about that. But I don't have any fitness strategy as such.'

'You only walk between your room and your balcony.'

'Don't I have to go to college?'

'I know you walk quite a lot from time to time. That's enough for you.'

'And I don't have any unnecessary calorie intake, unlike you people.'

'Did you scold me? Or did you convey that it's a nuisance to you?'

'Who am I to scold you? After all, I'm obliged to you for sharing…'

'Please, please, don't say these things again and again. I don't like it. Just as you need to share this flat, so do I. Why don't you view it like that?'

'Maybe you needed to at one time. But if you feel like, buy a flat or a bungalow of your own and shift there.'

'Maybe I can buy a medium-sized flat or a small house, but…'

'But what? You're unable to shift because you think I'll have a problem, isn't it?'

'You know everything, but that's not true, Achira.'

'Sorry.'

'No, *I'm* sorry; I didn't want to hurt you, believe me. That's the last thing I would do.'

'You can do everything, Dev. I think there's no limit. We are humans. And there's nothing on earth that humans can't do. Everything's possible.'

'So, you should consider the truth in every possible aspect of life.'

'Maybe I do, maybe I don't.'

'Just like you think your thoughts are true, don't always think that other people's thinking is false. You'll see every now and then that you have a completely different kind of experience.'

'Right now, other than doing my job, I mean teaching, I don't need to gain any experience in any special field.'

'And your writing? Is that your alter ego's business!'

'You can't argue about everything. And my writing didn't suddenly start now. I've grown up with these games and bygones. I don't think they will ever leave me.'

'That means that when you vehemently say that you've left everything of your past behind, it's not really true.'

'I came here with this same old flesh and blood that I'm made of. A bit of poison is mixed with that. Maybe that's what my *sadhana* is—the poison comes out of my body, bit by bit, through my tears, and I keep becoming purer.'

'Tinni, please don't talk like that; I feel terrible. I have lots to say to you. And there are even more things to hear from you. Will you get terribly angry if I cancel my trip?'

'Get angry? I'll go mad! I'll shift to the girls' hostel tomorrow. You'll never see me again in your life. You may be famous, you may be very powerful, but my own wishes are far dearer to me than that.'

'If you say one more nasty thing…'

'I don't want to say anything at all.'

'I'll fly away from this balcony just now; you'll see I've become Spiderman.'

'You won't do anything. It's getting time for you to leave; get ready.'

'There, Tinni's talking like a good little girl. What do you want me to bring back for you, Tinni?'

'If you have the time, bring a photograph of each of the places you visit. And after your return, sit on my balcony again and tell me stories about those places. Stories about Sumedha. Stories about Anandi. Stories about Shreya. Tell me about Rohini.'

'By the way, am I some storytelling granddad? And why did you say you want to hear about Rohini while you said you want to hear stories about all the others? Why the difference?'

'Because she's the only one I know. I've only heard about the others. Maybe that's why.'

'You know there's chocolate pie too. So let me tell you about it.'

'It's very sweet.'

'Do you know how to make salty pies?'

'Rohini used to make them—not exactly salty, but not too sweet either.'

'Then have some ice cream. After all, you like that.'

'I'll have it. In a little while.'

'When did you see Shounak last?'

'At the university convocation. I've talked to him over the phone a few times since then.'

'Was that when you went to present a paper?'

'Didn't he tell you?'

'Tell me what?'

'That he had come home on holiday then.'

'I think he met Shubro again a few days ago. But Shounak speaks highly of Shubhro. I mean, his intelligence, his approach to his career, and so on.'

'Maybe he has good reason to speak well of him.'

'But I think he has one problem.'

'I told you before, Dev, you don't know Shubro or anything about him, so I don't think it's appropriate for me to discuss him with you.'

'Alright, don't do it. But I do know you…'

'What do you mean by that? In the last two years and two or two-and-a-half months, you've seen little bits of me. Any words we exchanged were entirely out of courtesy. Before that, whatever Rohini told you was in regard to sharing a flat with somebody, and in order to assure a celebrity like you that you won't have any trouble. I need solitude for my wounds to heal, and you need to be away from crowds, that's all, that's the basis of knowing me. Isn't that a fair summary?

'It is.'

'I could claim so, but ultimately who's to say how genuine that is….'

'There's no need to say anything to anyone. And if you must say something, then address your question to this open sky of yours, to the intoxicating *madhavilata* and the impetuous wind.'

'Dev, please; is it very difficult for the rest of the world to leave me alone?'

'Ask yourself. After all, you have all the answers.'

'I know my destiny.'

'After all, you're the profound grandma.'

'I like the colour of your T-shirt very much.'

'Once more, once more. The color of what?'

'Your T-shirt.'

'Oho! My God, what a surprise!'

'What's there to be surprised about?'

'You observed something about me with your own eyes! What else but a surprise for me!'

'Why, don't I observe anything?'

'You look, you don't observe.'

'Rubbish.'

'Of course it's rubbish. You don't observe anything but yourself.'

'Because I can't see anything other than that.'

'Don't say you can't see anything. You turn your eyes away because you think your problems will be solved if you remain in solitude.'

'Whether it's solved or not, at least the problem won't grow larger, and that's a lot for me.'

'Maybe you're right in thinking that's the truth from your wasteland, but I think it's terribly wrong to give up trying to identify the possibilities within even that.'

'It's not as if I've given up everything.'

'Of course that's true, in one sense. That's why you look impossibly beautiful.'

'Don't talk rubbish.'

'Don't I have anything better to do than talk rubbish? Whoever has seen you for a little while likes you very much. Think for yourself—Leena, Suraj, me; everyone's your fan.'

'It's celebrities who have fans. But I'm…'

'But you're Achira. But you're Tinni.'

'Invite your parents to come here when you're back. Maybe they don't come thinking it'll be a problem for me.'

'Do you want to increase the number of your fans?'

'What rot you talk! Your Ma said that when they come, they stay in a hotel or meet you in Pune.'

'They do whatever is convenient for them. And I do have to visit Leena's parents in Pune. So, it becomes a family get-together. But there's no reason to think I lack any sense of responsibility. I make sure all the arrangements are taken care of.'

'It's Suraj who does all that.'

'He does. But how could Suraj do it unless I think about it?'

'I know you do!'

'Meaning? I never imagined that I'd get such appreciation today. I've thought about today for a long time.'

'That means it's no coincidence that you didn't go to Kihim Beach with your friends?'

'Don't interrogate me so much. You never know what might come up.'

'What might come up? That's the question right now.'

'Think about it; you have a month's time in your hands. Before you know it, the time will fly by.'

'As if I give a damn.'

'Of course you give a damn, Tinni; that's why you ask all the "what," "why," and "where" questions, and some more.'

'Can you smell something? It wafts in from far away, then wafts away and is gone. Maybe the breeze brings in the smell of incense that the devotees at the Haji Ali Dargah light.'

'It brings blessings for you. Be well, Achira. They say—be well, Tinni. Can't you hear it?'

'Do you love to talk?'

'Why, don't you? Didn't you like it today?'

'Maybe I did. But still…'

'"Still," "but," "although"… Do you derive great pleasure from using these words?'

'Perhaps my definition of pleasure is different from yours.'

'You think that you're doing something exceptional. That's what's special about you.'

'There's nothing special about me. And I don't have any inferiority complex about that.'

'We have plenty of other things to do besides argue to while away this evening. Do you want to listen to music? I have some country music, which you'll like. You'll enjoy hearing that.'

'Let's do something else; come let's cook.'

'Instant noodles? I don't want that.'

'No, not instant noodles. How about rice and fried fish?'

'That'll be great. But I've already ordered food from "Only Fish".'

'Why did you do that? Will you be able to eat more after all the stuff you just had?'

'Am I the only one eating? We'll eat that after midnight, on your real birthday.'

'I'm just not used to all this.'

'Why, haven't you ever had a meal after midnight?'

'Rarely. I can't remember the last time I did something like that.'

'You often go without food.'

'Who told you?'

'Why? You might as well admit that on the days I use the kitchen, you don't go there.'

'And so that means I go without food—how can you arrive at that conclusion so easily?'

'No, nothing's easy. Most difficult of all is your slough.'

'That's the only thing that I still have.'

'And what about the person inside?'

'If at all there's a person inside, she's so bloody that you could hardly recognize her as a human.'

'Nothing that's easy is nice. And it doesn't draw me.'

'"Naturals" ice cream is drawing me right now.'

'What are we waiting for?'

'Because we have nothing else to do.'

'Who said so? There are so many events all over the world. Is there ever any end to things to do?'

'My world means my job, my salary, the holidays, and teaching. Attending to all that will take care of the rest of my life. After I retire, hopefully, I'll have the money from my provident fund and insurance policy to go and stay somewhere near the sea. If I can manage to do that, I'll be content.'

'You want to go and live in Pondicherry.'

'It's definitely Rohini who told you that.'

'Yes. She asked me to find out about the place.'

'She asked you to find out?'

'Yes. If you don't believe me, you can ask her.'

'No. It's not that. But to tell you…'

'Sorry. No, Rohini wasn't talking about you. She said she had some plans regarding buying real estate in Pondicherry. Several people we know have homes there. They go there for holidays or plan to live there later. That's why she asked me to find out. She asked whether I, that is, Suraj, could suggest some properties.

That's what we spoke about one day.'

'The ice cream is truly nice.'

'Can anything be falsely nice?'

'Yes, of course. Those who have experienced that know what the greatness of falsehood means.'

'Maybe I'm also getting infected with a fear like you. I mean, suppose today suddenly disappeared. Then the whole thing would become a great lie.'

'I think so too. As if it's all bits and pieces of the stories of our lives.'

'But we wouldn't have been created without those bits and pieces of stories. They are absolutely necessary for a complete person to be built.'

'The difficulty is that the things you call bits and pieces of stories don't just build you; they break you too.'

'And from the breaking comes the possibility of building something new.'

'Philosophy.'

'Science as well.'

'Hey, the ice cream's melting.'

'But you didn't melt at all.'

'Water freezes and becomes ice; ice freezes and becomes wood.'

'One should know to bring down the sun. And once the sun comes down, the glacier descends, and after that, it's called a river.'

'And then it flows into the salty sea water.'

'I'll add ice cream and make it sweet.'

'Are you planning to buy the production facility of "Naturals"?'

'Tinni, didn't you have any boyfriends before you met Shubro?'

'Of course I did.'

'Who was your first boyfriend?'

'Are you talking about me having someone in the way you had Sumedha?'

'You needn't be so naive.'

'I didn't grow up in a big city like you; that's why, until a certain age, I was what you would refer to as naive. Most of the schools in the villages or mofussil towns were co-ed. So, to a large extent, I came of age without giving any separate importance to boys; rather, I grew up with them.'

'You with boys, I can't imagine that. Have you ever played cricket? Football?'

'We didn't know in our childhood that you couldn't become a boy unless you played cricket and football. At least at that time, the mingling of boys and girls in our mofussil town was not a very complicated matter.'

'I too studied in a co-ed school. Right from the time I was an infant until engineering college. With Sumedha in school and with Anandi in college. Is there any reason to think that only Sumedha and Anandi were in my class? Who all were with you? Do you still remember them warmly?'

'Like you had girlfriends, I didn't have anyone as such while in school. But in college…'

'After joining college, you were afflicted with the great lady!'

'No, it wasn't as if I didn't like Shubhro and was merely afflicted.'

'Didn't you have any spontaneous love other than that arranged affair?'

'I wonder why you're conducting so much research about me!'

'Besides wondering, there's also something called action; aren't you adept at that?'

'Very adept. I can twist your ears just now.'

'Please do that. There'll be some screaming then.'

'How long is your flight?'

'I think it's about eight hours.'

'Eight hours! Will you sleep all the way?'

'No. I'll dream.'

'Can you dream simply by saying so?'

'Anything's possible if really you want it.'

'Really?'

'Didn't you see, I wanted to celebrate your birthday with you, and that's it. All that came true somehow. Forget about all that; tell me about your first love.'

'I didn't have any first, second, or third love, nor do I have any now.'

'Okay, tell me when you first fell in love.'

'The day I entered the green paddy field to see grasshoppers and got lost.'

'Who was with you?'

'There was no one. But I had thought I ought to go with someone or the other. Who would bring me back.'

'The same green surrounds you even today. That's why your whole presence has the same liveliness. That attracts me immensely.'

'If I truly had any such capability, you wouldn't have found me here today.'

'Perhaps it's my fate to have been able to meet you. So, you would have had to come here. And the same is true for me too.'

'What fun you'll have! Visiting so many places…'

'Actually, I'll hardly have time for anything. After all, I'm going on a work-related tour. Will you come with me? We'll see many seas. Each one of them has a particular feature. The color of the water is different, the colour of the sand is different…'

'I used to lie in my room and dream about such things at one time. Now I don't even have the courage to do that. Sometimes I think that if I could get some kind of fellowship…'

'Why don't you try? You could very well get it.'

'Do you know how long it took Rohini to get one? And she had been trying for a long time. Of course, I doubt whether she would have gone at all if Samir didn't join her.'

'Samir too is very talented.'

'I'm very ordinary compared to them. My results were okay because I took my studies seriously. And that's why it was possible for me to get a job, so that I could at least feed myself.'

'You would definitely have started working under any circumstances.'

'Yes, I would have. I couldn't have sat at home.'

'So, the question of not liking the fact that you're working doesn't arise.'

'I never said that I don't like working. I never even thought about that.'

'Why don't you uproot the things that you don't like? Why do you retain all that as if they're an integral part of you?'

'There are some things that can't go. They can't be washed away. They have to be cast into flames. They'll leave with me. And then turn into smoke that disappears in the air.'

'Why don't you say something different today? About yourself, personal things.'

'All these are my personal matters. Like my mornings. And these amazing eyes.'

'Which morning?'

'Once, while visiting my Mashi's place, it was suddenly decided one evening that we would take the train that very night to go to Benares. We had two days, Saturday and Sunday, in hand. But try as he might, my Mesho was unable to get reservations in either the AC or first class. My Mesho worked in the railways. So, he got reservations for the 3-tier sleeper class. There were four of us, but we only had three berths.'

'May I light a cigarette? I'm dying to smoke. Your tale is creating a certain kind of situation. Please don't get angry. And then?'

'We boarded the train after a light dinner; I think it was about nine at night. Once we were on the train, we saw that the reserved coaches too were crammed with people. People sat wherever they found a bit of space. I had not traveled in an unreserved coach on an overnight journey before that. So, I was very scared.'

'By the way, how old were you then? I mean which class were you in, at school?'

'In Class 11.'

'So, you were quite grown up.'

'More than grown up.'

'What's that now?'

'That's Achira.'

'That's lightning.'

'It's like: *"meghomala shawne toritolota jonu / hirodoye shel dei gelo.* Dark patches of clouds accompanied by a lightning spiral / shot an arrow in the heart."'

'Please explain that to me.'

'There's nothing to explain. And if I really start explaining, it'll be like teaching a class.'

'Let it be that. But explain it, please. The words have a rhythmic cadence. Interesting. Tell me, what does it mean?'

'It's not the meaning that's important. As soon as you said lightning, I remembered an image and a line by a very famous poet. The two together. What power the poets of yore had to create images! A painting with words, a moving image simply with words—an amazing power!'

'But explain it to me first.'

'After waiting for long, Krishna saw Radha in a flash, and he reflected that seeing her amidst the darkest clouds of yearning was like lightning. The only light that was glimpsed. It was as if the light of Radha's beauty only sharpened his heart's anguish.'

'Why?'

'She was glimpsed like a flash of light. He could not see her properly in her full form. His yearning thus became even more fierce; his anguish only increased.'

'Great poet!'

'That's why he could express such an exceptional experience so well.'

'That's the advantage poets have—the poem can say just whatever the poet wants.'

'That's right.'

'Who first recited such a poem to you, Tinni.'

'I don't know.'

'Tell me, won't you tell me?'

'I don't remember.'

'I don't believe that.'

'Don't believe it.'

'Tell me the poem then.'

Jol pore, pata nore / tor kotha mone pore. Water drops, a leaf stirs too. I remember you.'

'Who said it?'

'You!'

'It's a topsy-turvy time! If only one could fetch a color good enough for you from the depths of the sea! So that I could hang it up on your wall!'

'My story got lost in the telling of this story! That's why Dushyant forgets everything.'

'And you think the fish will revive the memory of you?'

'No. The thinking changed.'

'Did Shakuntala find another meaning to her life?'

'I don't know if it was another or not. For the first time, she learned that living was for oneself. And so, her happiness was also something new. Her grief, too, was new.'

'Can someone know you, Tinni?'

'This is a question that all the people in the world could ask one another after spending some time together. And perhaps it's because such a question exists that even today people dream about being together.'

'Then why do you want to keep the question at such a distance?'

'My experience tells me that I can't bear to be terribly happy or sad. My thinking and consciousness are awfully middling.'

'In that case, I've never even heard about anything called thinking or consciousness!'

'Coming back to that story, you know, although the train compartment was so crowded, my cousin and I found a place on the upper berth. My Mashi was on the lower berth, and Mesho in the middle berth. My cousin and I had planned beforehand that we would chat all night long on the train.'

'Did you find someone on the train to talk to?'

'Arey Baba, no. We had so much to talk about. I was still not very familiar with the city of Kolkata. I did my schooling and grew up in a series of mofussil areas. My cousin was a bit younger than me. That's why she was interested in my tales. Besides, both of us liked reading storybooks and listening to songs. She used to tell me the stories of many films, complete with the dialogue. While my mother strictly prohibited me from going to the cinema, Mashi always took my cousin along to the cinema. I don't know why she did that. I still don't.'

'Didn't you ever go to the cinema in your childhood?'

'Rarely.'

'But I've seen plenty of films. My parents, Shreya, and I often went together to the theater during holidays.'

'Before I came to Bombay, I never knew that cinema halls were called "theaters", and I only began watching films after going to college.'

'Did you watch films with the great lady too?'

'Very few times, when I was in college.'

'And with her great son?'

'I did.'

'What?'

'See films.'

'You didn't complete the train story.'

'Maybe it's halted at the station.'

'Brilliant!'

'The whole night we were taking in whispers and giggling, and pretending to cough if it ever got too loud.'

'And after that?'

'Not after. In the course of doing that I discovered that, on the opposite berth, a pair of eyes was observing us and secretly listening to everything we said. But there was no blemish on those eyes that night. By then, one had learnt quite a bit to recognize the different kinds of looks and stares one got on the street. So, the eyes only increased our enthusiasm, not discomfort.'

'And then?'

'And then wings appeared on the horse's back, and it became the king of the skies.'

'Meaning?'

'There's no meaning.'

'Is that it—the end?'

'Where did it begin that it should end?

'But I still didn't get the story.'

'Do you think a story roams the streets? A story is something that slithers into the mind.'

'But what happened to the pair of eyes that you perhaps still search for all by yourself?'

'The massive train took him along that day, far away somewhere. I don't know. I still haven't heard from him. Only that morning became mine. The whole of Benares station that morning became mine.'

'Interesting.'

'Nothing was spoken. No words were exchanged.'

'But an amazing feeling can still be created sometimes.'

'I think the train was supposed to reach Benares at five in the morning, at dawn. It arrived late, at about seven. We got off the train and were standing on the platform. My Mesho went to look for a colleague. He was supposed to arrange for a guesthouse for us. The train was still standing at the platform. But who knows where those eyes were. I couldn't spot the person. I wished I could see him once before the train left. He would be lost. He didn't have a name. He lived somewhere far away.'

'Why didn't you ask for his name?'

'But I didn't see the need for that. And besides I can't speak to anyone of my own accord.'

'Does anyone know that better than me! What happened after that?'

'Nothing happened. After a while, the whistle also blew for the train to depart. Yet the eyes weren't to be seen. But I was really eager, if only I could see those eyes and that amazing, stricken gaze. The polite meek look that touches one deeply.'

'And there was no further encounter for the rest of your life.'

'That only came later.'

'So, what came earlier?'

'The train began moving slowly. Then I began to think that things like these keep happening in life, so what's so special about this one? I should feel happy about the trip now. And then suddenly, someone stuffed something into the palm of my right hand and jumped onto the train. That pair of eyes were then at the door of the moving train. He was moving away slowly. I was still in the state of being startled. By the time I opened my hand and looked, the eyes and the train itself had gone out of sight.'

'What did he give you? Let me guess, his address?'

'No. That's what I too thought it might be.'

'So, what did those eyes of yours give you?'

'Not my eyes, his eyes.'

'What was it then?'

'Éclairs! Four of them.'

'Éclairs! Why?'

'During that night-long chat, my cousin and I ate lots of chocolate éclairs. One after another.'

'Did you offer any to the eyes too?'

'No, no.'

'He gave you your favorite thing because he liked you.'

'Maybe, maybe not.'

'The eyes got lost because he got down at the platform and went looking for chocolates.'

'I think so.'

'Because he couldn't get anything else, he bought just the éclairs to give you.'

'Maybe. That's why the parting was sweet.'

'Wow! That was really nice.'

'I always say nice things.'

'That's completely true. But you say very little. You hardly want to speak.'

'It's because I say little that you still like me. Or else you would have no need or desire to talk to an ordinary person like me.'

'Everything finally leads to the same amazing thing, doesn't it, Tinni? I become a false person. Only my profession matters and my outward identity.'

'If I thought that was the only truth, then you wouldn't have been able to make me agree to have tea with you in the morning, or...'

'Or what, Tinni?'

'Oh, nothing.'

'It's going to be midnight shortly, your birthday dinner.'

'It's been going on ever since morning.'

'Tinni, do you still have those éclairs with you?'

'I think so.'

'I too like to fall asleep sometimes thinking about my childhood, or something nice that suddenly happened.'

'Every night, when I'm unable to sleep, I feel like reliving such feelings, which were true once but are no longer there now. But it's this return that's the real thing. Like loving that love.'

'What does that mean?'

'I'll tell you the meaning when you return after a month.'

'But didn't you tell me that we'd talk over the phone?'

'I said that if you called, I would speak to you. Where do I have the money so I can make overseas calls every day?'

'How mean!'

'It's a fact. Believe it or not.'

'I'll phone you! Don't try to find pretexts for not talking.'

'I'm hardly able to deal with my college texts. Where do I have the time to look for more?'

'What do you mean more?'

'Another text.'

'What's that?'

'Didn't you say I was looking for a pretext?'

'If you had been a lawyer, you would have made a name for yourself.'

'My Baba used to say that too.'

'Given the sharpness of your reasoning and interrogation.'

'That's why I am a lost cause.'

'I really want to make you victorious.'

'But if someone else makes you win, then that's only a defeat.'

'If one accepts your reasoning, then logically, one can say that if someone else makes you lose, then actually it's a victory.'

'Loss, victory, compensation… I guess that's what life is all about.'

'I don't think so. I don't believe it either.'

'Your beliefs didn't ever collapse into the dirt, float away in waters, or become one with the black body of darkness, and that's why your thinking and my feelings are not the same, because that's not possible.'

'Look ahead, Tinni, as far as one can see, there's only darkness laid out. Yet, you know that it's not a void. Beneath the darkness lies the blue sea. Above us, the sky has apparently hidden itself, it needs some sleep. Once it's morning, little by little, someone will dip a paintbrush in color and fill the whole canvas with colors. But the darkness will remain. Then comes it's turn to be concealed. But these colors wouldn't even be created unless that excess of darkness arrived. Can you see now, where your victory lies?'

'What do I know…'

'There's nothing on this earth that you don't know.'

'Don't make fun of me.'

'Although I'll be far away, I'll still be able to observe this way of looking of yours.'

'You…'

'You what? Do you know how many times I've delivered dialogues in this while… No, I won't tell you. I'll tell you the day you think of me as something other than a flirt.'

'I'm not compelling you in any way.'

'You don't do that. But you do something that…'

'Alright, this problem will be solved once I move out. That's easy too.'

'But you've moved to a new city. Why do you still find so many things difficult?'

'Your problems and mine are of a completely different nature.'

'By the way, I don't have problems.'

'What do you have then?'

'My happiness.'

'Wow! Well said! Yours is happiness, and mine is illness.'

'Even if it is illness, you ought to treat that.'

'Some illnesses can't be treated, and you know that too.'

'It's not about treating or not treating. The main thing is to reduce one's anguish.'

'Sometimes one finds oneself in the midst of living with the anguish.'

'The anguish that pricks you like a thorn every day—do you think holding on to that and hiding yourself away amounts to finding yourself?'

'Did you study clinical psychology?'

'I have to portray characters. I don't know anything. Why do you think a body is entirely dumb?'

'I don't think anything. I told you the same earlier; I'll say it again.'

'Don't say it anymore.'

'So I won't say it.'

'Nothing matters to you. If the person about whom I've thought a lot and think a lot doesn't care about that, there's one great advantage. I can think of the whole situation in my own way.'

'What do you do when you're alone?'

'A lot of things!'

'Like?'

'Like I listen to music, read books, cook, sleep, dream, do my research, smoke cigarettes, enjoy myself with my favorite drink, workout. You know about all that.'

'What do you mean I know?'

'You've seen me doing a lot of these things at home. Besides these, I also do a couple more things. I'll tell you about that later.

Not today. At exactly twelve, I'm going to kiss you.'

'Enough!'

'Just let go of your pride that you understand everything very well. You'll then see that you like the world around you sometimes.'

'Neither your popularity nor your fame will be affected in any way if you don't worry about what I like or don't like.'

'I didn't say anything blasphemous to you. The way you react!'

'Every person has their own yardstick of what's acceptable and what's not.'

'I know that.'

'Come and eat. You should rest a bit before leaving. Besides, you should check your things once.'

'"Only Fish" did not lay the table. We have to do that ourselves.'

'Tell me what you want?'

'Do you have the mauve tablecloth here?'

'Yes. Do you like that?'

'It's a beautiful colour. White crockery and golden cutlery!'

'I hope you don't miss your flight doing all that!'

'That'll be great!'

'Don't be childish!'

'Go to college tomorrow and ask for leave. After that, come along with me. You'll be able to meet Rohini. We'll visit Shreya too.'

'It seems you're going on a vacation. Will your dummy do all the work?'

'That would have been great!'

'Do I have to lay the table all by myself?'

'Not at all. Let me heat the food.'

'Why did you order so much food? You won't be here, so how long will I go on eating all this food?'

'Take out something and have that on the days you don't feel like cooking. You don't have to eat it again and again on consecutive days; that won't be nice.'

'What about inviting Leena over? She said she loves having *mocha*. She said she goes to "Only Fish" to have *dab-chingri* and *mocha*.'

'What do you love to eat most?'

'Chinese and Thai food. Not at a multi-cuisine restaurant, but where the cuisine is specifically Chinese or Thai. A woman cooks food and brings it to our college. I've never had such tasty food anywhere.'

'Let's have that one day. I, too, love Thai cuisine. Of course, I've had Chinese food since I was a child, so I don't like that so much now.'

'You surely must have tasted genuine Chinese cuisine too when you went to China?'

'Yes, I did that. But most of the herbs they use have a very strong smell, so I can't say I liked it very much. But I liked a few Japanese dishes a lot.'

'But I haven't even tried all the Indian cuisines.'

'Neither have I.'

'It's this fragrance of mung-dal that's special.'

'A completely Bengali fragrance.'

'Does it have no fragrance when the rest of India eats this dal?'

'God! Why should that be?'

'That's what it boils down to. In north India, dal means something like fried dal. It has onions, garlic, tomatoes, and pungent garam masala, which makes it impossible to discern the dal's own fragrance. In the south, they use coconut and tamarind instead. If sambar is prepared using masur-dal instead of tur-dal, would they know the difference?'

'Of course they would! Bengalis can't help rating themselves highly on all their matters.'

'Don't say they can't help it. Say they are capable and therefore confident about themselves.'

'I'm a complete fan of Bengalis. You could call me an admirer too.'

'So do things the way they ought to be done.'

'How are the prawns?'

'Nice. Very nice. Rohini loves prawns prepared this way.'

'Are you going to pack some for her?'

'If you were going there directly, you could have taken it along.'

'Given my schedule, it'll be at least fifteen days before I meet them. The prawns would turn into pickles by then. Have some more. You eat so little.'

'Don't say that. With all that I ate today and the quantity, I can go without food for the next week.'

'Are you on a diet?'

'I can't work if I eat too much. I just feel like sitting down. I can lie down and read a book or listen to music, but I don't feel like doing any writing or other work.'

'See how your regulations are all of the opposite kind. If a person has to do a lot of work, then she has to eat well too. Or else the calories would fall short.'

'But I don't have to do arduous work like you. That's why I don't realize anything. But I feel uncomfortable if I eat too much.'

'But you're eating so little now that I'm feeling uncomfortable.'

'I'm not going anywhere; you can eat as much as you like.'

'After I've eaten, I'll get éclairs for you.'

'No. You don't have to get anything more.'

'Then come with me to the airport. We'll buy éclairs on the way.'

'No. I'm going to fall asleep right here on the table.'

'But you often go without sleep.'

'You know everything, do you?'

'I know a little bit.'

'Have another prawn.'

'No.'

'I'll have some ice cream a bit later. I need to bring down the containers to keep all this.'

'You could leave it in these containers itself.'

'That'll take up too much space.'

'You can use my fridge.'

'Thanks. I'll do that if required.'

'You go and rest a bit. I'll clear the table.'

'It's you who needs to rest a bit. You have a long journey ahead of you.'

'I'm used to long journeys. Tell me, shall I take a holiday for a few days after I return?'

'Where will you go?'

'I won't go anywhere. I'll chat with you, and I'll cook and eat. I'll feed you, too. Will you be able to get a few days off?'

'It's tough.'

'Then it should be done!'

'Why?'

'Because you are the toughest, so tough jobs are only for you.'

'You don't let go of the slightest chance of pulling my leg, do you?'

'Because there's no chance of pushing you instead.'

'Just shut up!'

'Just a few more minutes now.'

'So you'll say whatever you like?'

'It's only talk. And in fact, I'm not saying even two percent of whatever I'd like to.'

'Keep the remaining ninety eight percent to yourself.'

'It's with me alright. Like caged lions and tigers in the zoo. Once they're let loose…'

'If you let them loose, they'll return to their cages at night to sleep.'

'Absolutely not.'

'That's what trapped creatures do most of the time in human society. By the way, are the curtains in your room going to be changed?'

'Suraj was saying something about that. I believe he spoke to you.'

'They were bought from the Refugee Handicrafts shop. I told Suraj that one day. But he didn't confirm.'

'Tell him to do that. I'll tell Suraj to give you a cheque. And get the car quickly. I'll go on a drive with you.'

'My car's monthly quota will be used up taking it to college and back. Who knows whether there'll be any chance of going on a drive.'

'Walk to your college sometimes. You'll have exercise. It's good for health.'

'I'm going to brush my teeth. You get ready.'

'Why don't you come with me? You don't have to get out of the car. I'll get off, and the car will drop you back.'

'No. You go alone. Be careful.'

'Why are you telling me all this right now? It's for later. When I leave. Ma used to say, *"gamane bamanaschaiva…"* etcetera, invoking Lord Vishnu as Vaman before a departure.'

'My Ma used to say, "Durga, Durga", invoking Ma Durga's blessings. And she forbade me from saying "I'm going." She used to say, "Say *I'm coming* all the time." The last time, I left saying "I'm going." But there was no prohibition, even in her eyes.'

'Will you say, "Durga, Durga" when I leave now?'

'I will.'

'Thanks. Suraj comes with a tilak on his forehead of vermillion, turmeric, and rice. I miss these Indian things when I'm far away.'

'I hardly think of all these things nowadays. In my childhood, I couldn't even think of beginning any task without turning to my parents.'

'It's normal that as you grow up, it wanes.'

'Becoming less is normal, not stopping altogether.'

'That's an exception that proves the rule! Let me get changed. Will you come along?'

'No. I won't go today; I'll go another day.'

'Okay. I'll keep that assurance.'

'Check your luggage once more. See if the plug points are turned off.'

'I'll check that. Please check once again when you get the time.'

Chapter 9

How shall I get out of this circle? God, I've forgotten to know you in a special way. I only wanted to find you in everything of mine, night and day. Sometimes it occurred to me that Rohini was an incarnation of my God. And sometimes this balcony. The freedom to wake up in the middle of the night and sing. But why is Dev becoming restless about me? How can this be stopped? I am only a good feeling for him. Perhaps only a bland story in the twists and turns of his life. But why do I feel restless even when I know all this? Why do I feel like escaping? I must start thinking seriously about the fellowship. I don't think it'll be easy to carry on like this anymore. Why have I still not grown up? If I had grown up, all these thoughts wouldn't have troubled me anymore. I wish Rohini was with me. But doesn't Rohini have anything else to do other than take care of me? She, too, wouldn't like it if I kept intervening in her life. Maybe she won't say anything, but I should realize that. Rohini, please forgive me. I have to leave this place too and go somewhere far away. Where will I go? Where can I go? I won't go anywhere. The blue of this sea has saved me. I won't abandon it and go anywhere else. I'll string words together and create a garland out of them. Saying it to myself, hearing myself. This sea has been witness to the many nights I was indebted to the sky. The dangling body of the sky lifted all the load off my body. It was on this balcony that I spread out my arms in the gentle breeze. I shivered in the embrace of countless winds. Can I afford to be excited like this? Achira, why didn't your shackles turn into anklets yet? After all, there can be no liberation for you unless you can play the pain…Who knows, maybe this feeling itself signals that playing. I must nurture it carefully and tenderly.

'Tinni, Tinni…'

'Don't call me that.'

'Tell me, how should I call you then?'

'You look very nice in that white shirt.'

'Then let me get rid of all my shirts of other colors. And let there be the greatest collection of white shirts in my wardrobe.'

'When it comes to nice things, the fewer, the better. It's not me, but my favorite poet who said that.'

'Your poets have said everything there is to say. Please tell me what I should do now. If everything I say sounds like an old hat to you, that's the fault of your poets, not mine.'

'What did my poets do now?'

'They occupy you entirely, isn't that correct?'

'That's not at all correct. But unless they're there, my existence too becomes dull—tasteless, rough, completely dry.'

'I think the car's arrived.'

'Are you ready?'

'The luggage is ready. I'm not ready. Yes, come in, Shinde. I have a lot of luggage this time—five items in all. Please take the four large ones; I'll take the hand luggage.'

'And Suraj sir?'

'Suraj will come directly to the airport in his car.'

'Okay sir. Good night, Madam.'

'Good night.'

'The keys and checks are on my desk. All the contact numbers are in the diary left there. If you can't get me on the phone, call Suraj, and I'll get the message very soon.'

'We never talked like this before you set off somewhere.'

'Because it's different this time, isn't it?'

'Why should it be different?'

'Because it's your birthday today.'

'I've also spent two previous birthdays in this very flat with you around. But there was none of this.'

'I'll bring back lots of seas for you. Don't scold me.'

'Be well.'

'Write to me. I'll wait for your emails.'

'Waiting requires time, which you won't have at all on this trip.'

'I'll have it. Do write.'

'Don't be late.'

'Then let me cancel my departure.'

'I meant don't be late now.'

'Are you very sleepy? Go to bed as soon as I leave.'

'Okay.'

'Won't you say, "Durga"?'

'Yes, I'll say it.'

'When?'

'Just when you exit the door.'

'May I request something?'

'Ask for something that I can agree to. Or else, I'll feel bad that I could not respond to your request.'

'If you haven't fallen asleep, say "Durga" once at my take-off time.'

'Do you believe in all this?'

'I do and I don't. But today I really want to believe. If the plane crashes midway, I won't be able to see you again. I have so much to tell you, I won't be able to say all that. I have so much to hear from you, I won't be able to do that. I can't bear to lose that. That's why it's good to have the power-pack of your "Durga".'

'But such things are largely based on faith. I've lost that faith, and so will my prayers have that strength anymore?'

'If *you* pray, everything will come true. That's my belief; it's what I feel.'

'Alright, I'll do that.'

'Tinni, I'm taking all your unhappiness with me. Be well. Become even more beautiful. Wait for me. You'll do that, won't you? You have the time to wait.'

'You're getting late.'

'May I…'

'Please, Dev…'

'Be well, be well.'

'Durga… Durga… *Gamane bamanaschaiva…*'

'See you. I'll miss you. Please miss me a little bit too.'

Chapter 10

I'm all alone in this flat after quite a long time. Why am I feeling like this? The day Rohini left, I felt a terrible void. There was a reason for that, too. But Dev's being here or being away didn't matter to me at all, all this while. He has left with all the lights on. Now, I've got to turn them off. Why does he want me to do this? His fame and prestige and everything touch the sky. He doesn't lack girlfriends. His relationship with his colleagues is also according to his wishes. That's what Rohini had said—that he's an expert in steady as well as casual relationships. She told me I should not behave like a moral policeman. She said that's how their lifestyle is, and so on. I never intervened even once in their lives. Then why is Dev keen on me? Because I live my life differently? Or is it because I carry a wound; to try to help me heal; to provide social assistance? Why me when there are so many others? Because he has me close by, in front of his eyes, that's why. I'm very weak compared to them, so that's why he's so keen to help me. It's much better to die than to be proven to be weak before someone. Shubro, too, considered me to be weak and treated me as he wished. There, I'm getting into the cesspool of all kinds of old memories. I can't let this happen under any circumstances. I never felt this way regarding Rohini. Maybe I just didn't have the capacity to feel anything then. Who's that calling now? This late? Must be Dev. No. I'm not going to receive his call, no way. I have to explain to him how important it is for me to be alone. Why is the phone going on ringing? It's Rohini. So late?

'Why so late at night, dear?'

'Just like that.'

'It's daytime there now, isn't it?'

'Were you writing?'

'No.'

'I hope you're well.'

'Yes, I'm very well.'

'I rang you up to wish you! Happy Birthday! But you sound… a bit disturbed. It's okay, you rest. I'll call you again later.'

'No, I can talk now. In fact, I really wanted to talk to you.'

'Why? What happened? Something in Kolkata?'

'No, nothing like that. Will you mind terribly if I look for paying guest accommodation?'

'I'll be unhappy. Listen, I'm confirmed in my job now. So, I can easily pay the bank's monthly instalments entirely by myself. You don't need to have the slightest worry about living in the flat.'

'Listen, it's not about the money.'

'The problem is sharing the flat with Dev, isn't it?'

'Mostly.'

'I could guess that, to some extent. His lifestyle is so different. I wouldn't have been able to adjust to that either.'

'It's not adjusting or not adjusting; that's the problem, Rohini. It's been almost two and a half years, did I ever complain about any problem?'

'No. So what happened suddenly now?'

'Nothing's happened.'

'If you don't want to talk about it, I'm not going to force you. But don't think of being a paying guest or anything like that. And listen, Dev will probably buy his own flat somewhere around Juhu and shift there. You'll be alone then. And when we visit, we'll stay with you.'

'Are you sure that Dev will shift soon?'

'He hasn't told me yet. I heard about it from Shreya.'

'In that case, don't tell them anything.'

'What should I not tell them?'

'That I told you all this.'

'But in all the conversations I had with Dev, I didn't get the impression that he had any problems regarding you.'

'I don't think I create any problems.'

'In fact, Dev thinks highly of you. Whatever Shreya told me about you, Dev had a lot of positive input in that.'

'That's where the problem lies.'

'Did Dev ask you anything about Shubhro or your time in Kolkata?'

'He knows Shounak who was in our college.'

'He told me about Shounak too. He visited us just recently. Shounak knows us somehow, through Samir's job. Shounak has some professional dealings with Shubhro too, but I didn't know that. Dev told me.'

'When did you talk so much with Dev?'

'In the last twenty hours.'

'What do you mean?'

'He probably found out about my birthday from you.'

'Exactly.'

'For the last twenty hours, I had to celebrate my birthday with him.'

'Oh! That's great! I should thank him!'

'But you know me.'

'I do; I know you don't like all that any more. But I'm not with you either, so if Dev makes the time to celebrate your birthday, that's wonderful. Given how busy he is—the last twenty hours! I can hardly believe it! I'm sure he was alone.'

'Yes.'

'So, what did he do? He's a wonderful cook. The last time he was here—at Shreya's place—he cooked lots of things over the two days and fed us. Wow! I'm really happy!'

'I was also happy, but I feel very uncomfortable now. I'm feeling annoyed with myself.'

'Don't feel annoyed about a birthday celebration. Listen, go to sleep now. I'll call you again after I return from work. Are you going to college tomorrow? I mean today?'

'I'll go. I have to submit exam papers today.'

'Okay. A good night to you.'

'Better to say good morning! Okay, bye. Take care.'

'Bye, thanks.'

It'll be morning soon. But I need to sleep too. I have to go to college today. I have to get out of the flat. I can't let this restlessness grow. There's not a single person in Bombay now whom I can talk to. The same old talking and talking. The bother of finding someone to listen. No. I have to get out of all this. Who's calling again now? Must be Dev. He must have reached the airport. Should I talk to him?

It'll be childish if I don't talk. That won't be appropriate, since it's my birthday.

'Yes. Tell me.'

'Not asleep yet?'

'No.'

'What happened, Tinni? Why does your voice sound like

that? Are you feeling unwell?'

'No. I'm alright. What about you?'

'I'm fine. I miss you a lot. Go to sleep. You have to go to college.'

'Where are you?'

'I just boarded the plane.'

'Take care.'

'Say, "Durga". I'll call you when I reach.'

'I'll probably be in college then.'

'You don't have to receive it. Just to let you know I've reached.'

'Be well. Bye.'

'Bye, dear. Take care. I will be there whenever you miss me.'

'Thanks.'

Come and get me, oh Sleep. I need you badly tonight. Come to me now. Please don't be far. Come to my glass of water, oh contentment. Sleep is my darkness. My hiding place. Good night, everything and everybody. Good night to me.

Chapter 11

'Hello, Tinni, can't you hear me?'

'Yes, tell me.'

'I didn't get the chance to talk to you all day. Sorry. Talk to me.'

'I'm fine. You?'

'Missing you terribly. Have you eaten?'

'Don't you have anything else to ask me?'

'I have lots of questions. I'm getting confused. I really wish I could see you. Where are you, on the balcony?'

'No. In my room.'

'Reading?'

'No. I'm not doing anything.'

'Missing me?'

'Not at all.'

'But I'm sure you're missing me.'

'What time does your show start?'

'At nine at night. But you'll be busy then.'

'So will you.'

'But I'm still with you now; that's how I feel. You're enjoying being alone, aren't you? What happened in college today?'

'Classes. Submitting examination papers. Paper-checking. Sitting in the staff-room. All that.'

'Nothing special?'

'No chance.'

'Then again, Dev is special.'

'So are you.'

'What color today?'

'The color of the sea is blue.'

'Which shade of blue?'

'I don't know. See it when you're back.'

'Really? Shall I come down?'

'That's up to you.'

'And nothing's up to you.'

'No, it isn't.'

'Can you go and stand on the balcony, please?'

'Why?'

'Tell me the colour of the sea in the darkness.'

'Everything's black like the color of my sari.'

'See, you could have told me that first. You wore a black sari. Why's that, are you unhappy?'

'No.'

'But I feel like you are.'

'Don't you have anything better to do?'

'Lots of work.'

'Finish your work. Or else you'll be late. I have to prepare notes for my class.'

'I'll talk to you later. Sleep well.'

'Okay. Bye.'

'Bye. See you soon.'

'You're right next door; you can easily drop in.'
'Try asking me. After all, it's only a matter of a few hours.'
'Do your work well. Bye.'
'Good night.'

Chapter 12

When Shubhro first began travelling abroad for a few days, waiting for his return was a strange kind of experience. Since I had prepared myself, his absence didn't cause much anguish. But there was no change in his demeanor. Each time, I used to eagerly await his return, but he was oblivious to that. Or did he ignore me deliberately? I used to rearrange our room; so much thinking and planning would go into what I would cook, but if he landed in Kolkata in the evening, it was late night by the time I saw him. And after coming home, how strange his behavior was! As if the few days' absence didn't have any meaning or significance for him. But why am I thinking about all this now? Is it because Dev's behavior is completely different? Did I wish for such behavior from Shubhro? But hadn't I forgotten about my anguish from those days? I'd begun to realize that it was because a person's life was not perfect, like a picture that she had to paint, sometimes with a brush and colors, and sometimes with words. And thus begins her emancipation and her growth. Why is Dev making me worry so much? Because I'm worried! I should tell Rohini everything. But why should I feel the need for someone like her all the time? Why should my *tapasya* be in vain time and again? I'm extremely weak. I should give some love to myself; Rohini was absolutely right. Why can't I love myself? I felt fulfilled merely by my own existence. But this restlessness hasn't scorched me like this in the last two years. I must immerse myself more in my reading and writing. I think the fellowship is vital. Will that rid me of these problems? Who'll tell me that? Rohini? She said she'd call me. But she didn't. She has so much to do. There I go, waiting once again. I need to be strong. Is it possible to obtain that strength externally? The phone…

'When are you coming to Bombay?'

'Why, dear, are you depressed? Why don't you do something? I'll send you the ticket; come and stay with me for a few days.'

'No!'

'Don't say no. I'm in a new job. It'll be tough to get any leave for the next six months. Take a fortnight's break and come over.'

'No, I can't burden you again and again.'

'Cut the bullshit! I know Dev must have told you something that triggered anguish. I can understand. Listen, if you think it's Dev who's the problem, then tell him directly that you're finding it inconvenient.'

'I tried telling him that several times.'

'Don't try. Tell him straight away. You're not obliged to talk to him or anything. Listen Achira, don't ever think again that for so-and-so reason you have to accede to and act according to the demands of such-and-such people, all in the name of good behavior.'

'It's the same old ailment of mine. Becoming submissive and just watching. I'm scared. There was the same kind of repeated misunderstanding with Ma'am too.'

'Don't do all that any more. If I speak to Dev about it, that would be childish.'

'But Dev suddenly…'

'You're completely different from the world he's seen; maybe that's the main reason for his attraction. Maybe he views you as a creature from another planet.'

'But whether intentionally or otherwise, I never felt any interest in him. I hardly have enough time to manage my own affairs.'

'Hey, what news about the book?'

'I'm looking at the second proof.'

'That means it'll be out in a few months.'

'I think so.'

'Listen, my Didi met Kaku and Kakima. She said she talked to them for about ten minutes. But apparently, they didn't enquire about you at all. Hey, are you there? Do you want to talk to them? On the phone?'

'No.'

'Alright, when you feel like talking, do that. I have their new number. Bye. I'll talk to you later. Don't be angry with me. Shubro's Ma misreported the whole matter to them. She's the one who's most happy that you're angry with your parents and don't have anything to do with them.'

'I'm really sleepy now.'

'Don't take too much medication.'

'No.'

'Try to apply for leave tomorrow itself.'

'Not so soon.'

'Then when?'

'After a few days.'

'Okay. Try to be cheerful. Take a walk on Marine Drive. You'll like it.'

'So late at night?'

'But we used to go even later, remember?'

'That's because you were here.'

'I'm still there. Take a deep breath; you'll feel my fragrance. What happened? Why are you crying? Haven't I told you that your quota of tears in this life is over? Did you wear a new sari on your birthday?'

'No. I didn't buy any new sari.'

'Okay. What present did Dev give you?'

'Lots of flowers, chocolates, and he ordered lots of food.'

'Wow! Please buy four saris on my behalf tomorrow itself.'

'I've bought a *kalakshetra* sari for you.'

'You could have sent it through Dev.'

'Yes, I could have.'

'Okay. Come along very soon with the sari. The next Fulbright application call will come out anytime now. I'm sure you'll get it this time.'

'Who knows, I've been thinking of applying to S.O.A.S. as well.'

'Just do whatever you want to do. And make sure you never do what you don't like to do, whatever the circumstances.'

'How's Samir? Terribly busy?'

'As usual.'

'I'll give him this book once it's out.'

'And you won't give it to me.'

'I will. First to him and then to you.'

'You're completely crazy. You're still the same.'

'As long as I have this lunatic asylum, I can stay that way, isn't it?'

'That's yours for life. Unless you leave and go away.'

'Please forgive me; I seem to have made it a habit to trouble you and make you unhappy.'

'I'm telling you, I'll start weeping now. I hope you've had dinner.'

'Yes. Be well.'

'You too.'

Chapter 13

Rohini was surely my Ma in an earlier life. And in this life, she cared for me like I was a little child and kept me alive. She understands me so well. I'm the one who doesn't. Perhaps that's because she loves me. But so do Ma and Baba. I never for once imagined that Baba wouldn't understand my plight. Their notion of "society"—who does that consist of? Am I not part of that society? Damn, I don't like to remember all that. Henceforth, I mustn't do what I don't like. Is there anything greater than the refuge of sleep? There isn't. Goodnight to me.

'Dev?'

'Why? Did you forget the sound of my voice?'

'The sound of your voice echoes in the ears of all the women of India. Is there any way they can forget it even if they want to?'

'No. For the last few days, I was so busy that I couldn't call you at a time that would have been suitable for you.'

'Do you know what time is suitable for me?'

'I know roughly when you have classes, when you go to sleep, and so on. Were you asking a complex question?'

'I'm the one who's complex.'

'I know. But not entirely.'

'Meaning?'

'The meaning's gone for a walk.'

'Where to?'

'Along the edge of the Mediterranean Sea.'

'Really?'

'When I'm there, you don't even notice me. But my being far away has made you remember me, at least a little bit.'

'Not even a little bit.'

'I don't think that's true.'

'Your real estate agent has given me some papers. Where should I send those?'

'Suraj will send someone to collect it.'

'And if I'm not at home then?'

'Are you planning to go out of Bombay during this period?'

'No.'

'Then he'll call you before coming from Suraj's office. He'll only go when it's convenient for you.'

'How are your shows going?'

'As they should.'

'Good.'

'See, I'm beginning to talk like you.'

'What do you mean like me?'

'Everything doesn't need to have a meaning.'

'Right.'

'This too?'

'Yes. This too.'

'Are you in the kitchen?'

'How did you know?'

'I could smell it.'

'Smell what?'

'The green coriander leaves.'

'You're wrong. It's the pungency of red chilies.'

'No. It's the smell of fenugreek's unhappiness.'

'What's to be done then?'

'Grind some turmeric, add some yogurt, apply that to your face, and keep it for a while; you'll feel better.'

'Very funny.'

'There, didn't I tell you. You were waiting to know the recipe for being cheerful. You could have called me sometime.'

'I wasn't waiting for anything at all.'

'Okay, you weren't, but Tinni was.'

'Tinni went to wet her feet in the sea.'

'All by yourself?'

'No.'

'Who did you go with?'

'The soft sunlight of evening and the surging wind.'

'I miss you terribly.'

'I got a dummy copy of my new book today.'

'Dedicated to Samir.'

'How did you find out about that?'

'Samir told me. Of course.'

'Networking.'

'Yes, Ma'am.'

'Okay, bye.'

'What happened? Are you angry with me or with Samir?'

'Why should I be angry with Samir?'

'Then with me?'

'No.'

'But I know ten million ways to deal with anger.'

'Deal with your twenty million fans' anger, please.'

'But my fans are never angry.'

'So?'

'So they've been stored carefully for those who aren't my fans, those who're always angry. What did Shubhro do when you were very angry?'

'He never did anything.'

'Okay. Who used to talk first once the anger had died down?'

'Any anger as well as affection was almost entirely one-sided, on my part alone. Shubro lived in his own world.'

'What world was that?'

'His study, job, seminars, and maybe there was more. Which I didn't know about in the initial few years.'

'And once you found out?'

'It was a bit too late.'

'But he courted you for quite a long time. What happened then?'

'At that time, thanks to Ma'am's personality, I never got the chance to think about anything else.'

'You didn't try to think about anything else?'

'No, I didn't. Results, career, an easy way to become known—because all that was right in front of me, I never wanted to look deeper.'

'Why did it take you so long to understand Shubhro's interests? You're so sensitive; why didn't you realize?'

'It's not that I didn't do anything at all. I thought everyone wasn't the same. And I thought it was his indifference that needed to be worked on.'

'What do you mean?'

'I thought that loving someone meant encircling him with everything I possessed. If he wanted to keep some distance, let him. But I would watch over everything.'

'And then?'

'After that, I gradually started to realize that the more the sphere of my encirclement spread, the more he moved himself away from it.'

'But did he have any other relationship?'

'He didn't, as far as I know.'

'Then what was it?'

'That's how he is. He can't bear any ties. He's not interested in anything for very long. Even in his academic career, he couldn't stick to any particular field. The same is true of his job.'

'I heard his knowledge on many subjects is outstanding.'

'That's right.'

'I heard he's working on linguistics now. With a biophysics approach.'

'I don't know. I'm not that updated.'

'I had a long chat with Shounak just yesterday.'

'Oh!'

'Shubhro's mother is a bit strange.'

'Why?'

'She lives with Shubhro now.'

'She too has millions of seminars and lectures in various countries.'

'I heard she went for Shubhro's treatment.'

'Must be.'

'Don't you want to know about what happened to Shubhro?'

'No.'

'Why not?'

'I have no desire to know.'

'Sorry.'

'There's nothing to be sorry about. I don't have any time now to think about anyone but myself. I just don't want to.'

'Tinni, shall I get you a scarf? The women here wear that, it looks lovely.'

'Bring it for those who wear it. It'll look nice on them too. I don't wear scarves anymore. I'll talk to you later. I'll be late if I don't finish my cooking quickly.'

'Late for what? Are you going somewhere?'

'No.'

'Then?'

'I'm not in the mood for such talk.'

'I made you unhappy by talking about Shubhro, didn't I?'

'Not unhappy. I don't like talking about my wounds with you or with anyone else.'

'Why are your wounds still raw, Tinni? Why does it still cause you pain?'

'Where's the pain? It just makes me uncomfortable.'

'But there could still be something you like relating to Shubhro.'

'Of course there is. But now I realize that I would feel the same way even if it was someone else instead of Shubhro.'

'I couldn't exactly understand you.'

'You don't have to understand everything. It's for grown-ups.'

'Is that so? Explain it to me when I return grown up in a few days.'

'I can only do that if I have the time.'

'Why? Where will your time go?'

'Can one say that in advance? Where does time have the time for that?'

'Shackle time with memories of me. You'll see how still it stands then!'

'I can't do that anymore.'

'Why not? Did the city suddenly wake up?'

'It was awake. Some people were looking for the concealment of sleep.'

'So, you're going to teach at S.O.A.S.?'

'I haven't decided yet.'

'Do you want to escape?'

'No.'

'Have the clouds disappeared after the curtains in my room were changed?'

'No. They didn't feel like it either.'

'That's right. How can they when the flat's so vacant and everything's spread out! It's best for them to confine themselves to the balcony and room.'

'I took out the *mocha* from the fridge today.'

'I had a terrific chicken sizzler today.'

'There are four parcels and about ten magazines for you.'

'Open it. You'll see Dev. Lots of pictures.'

'If I feel like it, I'll do that.'

'What are you reading now?'

'*Lipika.*'

'Written by your lover?'

'Yes.'

'Is it No. 1 or No. 2?'

'So cheap.'

'You can have several lovers, but if I say that I become cheap.'

'I never said anything like that.'

'Make fruit punch and drink it; you'll feel cheerful. After I return, I'll teach you how to prepare several kinds of mocktails.'

'I can make do with whatever I know.'

'Make a different one each time when you invite me.'

'High hopes!'

'Hopes should be high. My father used to say that one should have lots of hope in store so that at last half of them can come true.'

'Whatever you wish.'

'I'd like to summon the sun to your balcony. I want the nights to be starry. I want you to deck your hair with colorful flowers. I want to bury my face in your bosom.'

'Shounak has possessed you.'

'The words are Shounak's.'

'I know.'

'But the poem is mine.'

'Good.'

'Just good?'

'What else? Very good.'

'You're only using elementary school adjectives.'

'My knowledge is limited to elementary school. What can I do?'

'If it were Shounak, you would have said lots of things.'

'Maybe so, maybe not.'

'I know how to say it.'

'You know a lot. I don't. There's no point arguing.'

'Samir gets a whole book while I can't even get a poem in return for mine.'

'The book is about Samir. Do you know that?'

'I know. But write one about me.'

'I'm not such an accomplished writer that it can be done at the drop of a hat.'

'But.'

'But Samir never asked me to write about him. I felt like doing it; that's why I tried to write it. It's not just about the animate Samir. The way I came to know him as a person—that's what inspired me to write something. Even if something about Samir arose, that was finally my interpretation, my analysis. It's not entirely Samir either. My thoughts and feelings became entangled in such a way that even if Samir reads it himself, I don't know how much of himself he'll find in the book.'

'Will you ever write about me?'

'I can't tell you that now.'

'You know, Samir is really excited. He's looking forward to reading the book.'

'Who told you that?'

'Samir did.'

'I really wanted them to be there at the book release.'

'But Rohini has a new job, and so she couldn't make it. Please have the release event after I'm back. Please, please.'

'If you release it, of course, quite a few books will get sold on the first day itself.'

'Now who's doing the leg pulling?'

'My publisher may get alarmed initially, but he can't imagine, even in his wildest dreams, that I would make such a proposal.'

'Why's that?'

'He'll think I've gone mad after writing just four books. Or that there isn't a greater fool than me on the soil of India.'

'Why? Why?'

'Why would he think of inviting a person like you to my book release event?'

'What if I speak to your publisher?'

'Will that be very good for me?'

'Why? After all, you're not so insubstantial as to be affected by any gossip.'

'I myself don't exactly know whether I'm insubstantial or substantial. And how would you know?'

'Let me get Suraj to handle the whole thing. He's the best person to do that.'

'My work is of an extremely humble nature.'

'Why should it be humble?'

'It's of a humble nature. I didn't say it was of humble quality. So, isn't it better that I conduct it at my own pace?'

'That's true. But I really want to do it.'

'Look, if I now feel that I should inaugurate your film, that would be just as inappropriate as you being there at my book release event.'

'Neither is inappropriate.'

'That would only be a false assertion. I never had Ma'am or even Shubhro attending my book release. And Ma'am or Shubhro were the financiers of my book at that time. But as far as they were concerned, it was just like giving me pocket money. So, they were never interested in finding out whether I ate phuchkas or Chinese food with that money. As soon as I wrote something, I used to want to read it out to Shubhro. But he'd say, "I'll read it once it's published." When I gave it to him after publication, he would say, "Keep it on the table. I'll look at it later." But he never got around to it. Even though he was always reading something or the other. Those were all on weighty subjects and discourses. I wasn't competent to occupy any space there. I only relied on my love. I had thought that as long as I loved, not half but the whole world would be mine.'

'But Tinni, the world is indeed yours. However much we joke about your balcony and room, the fact is that you live in an extremely large world.'

'Sorry, Dev, I wasted a lot of your time by intruding into your work time.'

'Don't be so diffident all the time. Do whatever you want, whenever you want. And think about whether the publisher can be approached about the book release.'

'Do your work mindfully. I'm hungry now. We'll talk again later.'

'Leave some for me. I'll have it when I'm back.'

'No way.'

'Alright. Don't keep it. Be well. Bye.'

'Bye.

Chapter 14

I said so much about Shubro today. Dev is doing all this intentionally. Let him. But hey, I don't feel so irritated today, neither for discussing Shubhro nor for Dev's outlandish thoughts. Good. That means I'm growing up. I must talk to Samir. Will he come by himself? No, it's better not to propose something like that. Again, the same old good or bad. The cooking turned out really well. I thought it would all be ruined because I was talking to Dev. That means I can do several things at once. Multi-tasking, as Rohini would say. Good, Achira; you've done a good job!

I have to sort out my books. I'm not dusting them regularly. Am I turning lazy? Or am I growing old? I'm not being able to handle everything. But no one else can arrange the books on my behalf. I shouldn't leave any work for Saturdays and Sundays. But the article I'm writing also pulls me in. I have to complete it. And if I'm to go to S.O.A.S., I'll need to prepare for that afresh. No one asks any questions at all over here. I'm the one who asks the question and also provides the answers. Where do they have so much time to think about one subject? All of them do so many other things besides their studies—hobbies, jobs, orientation courses, part-time employment, preparing for professional training—that they don't have time to form questions. They only need to pass the examinations. If I mutter to myself too long, I won't be able to sleep. So, my dear doorway, I'll see you again tomorrow morning. There's a door, but where's the doorway? Maybe it exists because it isn't there. And if it were there, it would be invisible. God! Now, oh Sleep, with you only...

'Is it you, Dev?'

'No. A ghost.'

'I'm extremely scared of ghosts. And the future too.'

'But your present...'

'My present is imprisoned by two hundred exam papers.'

'Not at all. How did you go to Ganpatipule?'

'In a vehicle hired by the college.'

'But you didn't tell me.'

'You didn't ask me.'

'Must one ask about everything?'

'No.'

'Then?'

'I don't think I signed any charter that I have to tell you everything.'

'Nor was it decided that you won't tell me.'

'Besides, you've spread your magic all over the world. All news has to make its own way to you. So, what does it matter whether I tell you or not?'

'You only thought of the news? You forgot about my wishes.'

'Thanks to my wishes, just below my balcony, a pair of bougainvilleas have sprung up from stone with all their thorns. Magenta and yellow, a mixture of the two colors. I'll show it to you when you return.'

'Is it high tide or low tide now?'

'Both.'

'How can that be?'

'It happens. One on either side.'

'I've bought a lampshade for you. And some junk jewelry.'

'But I don't wear all that.'

'Decorate your room with it.'

'How did you know about all this?'

'Through my mind.'

'But I haven't bought anything for you.'

'Did I ask you to?'

'Can't say. You might as well ask. You might think I went somewhere and didn't get anything for you.'

'A mountain on one side and the sea on another…'

'What's that?'

'Ganpatipule. A lot like you. Did you write something?'

'I don't have very much to do besides that. I read quite a bit too.'

'And what did your students do?'

'They had fun in their own way—singing, dancing, being offended, quarrelling. We had a lot to eat as well.'

'Did you enjoy it, going in a group like that?'

'It wasn't so bad either.'

'Did you find something to write about?'

'Do you think I am a full-fledged writer, or what? Nor did anyone send me on a writing mission. I'm a very ordinary person.'

'All people are ordinary people.'

'No, not at all… I got the chance to stay with such a big shot that I have no difficulty knowing my own place.'

'Did you speak to the publisher?'

'Yes, next week a final dummy of the book will reach Samir.'

'Won't you send me one?'

'See it when you return.'

'Can't I read it?'

'Where do you have so much time? It's not so easy to read a three hundred page novel.'

'Do you think only you can do difficult things?'

'I'm good for nothing.'

'Such humility isn't good. You can do lots of things, and again, there are lots of things you can't do. And that's normal.'

'Whatever it is, knowing that I'll get one more reader may make this a happy journey; what do you say?'

'Suraj had a preliminary discussion with your publisher.'

'What discussion?'

'He didn't mention you. I think you're feeling embarrassed about that.'

'It would have been better not to get into all this.'

'Please, Tinni, there's nothing I've done or will ever do that causes you inconvenience in any way. I give you my word.'

'No one kept their word. No one keeps their word.'

'Dev is not no one.'

'I know.'

'You don't know anything.'

'I know, Dev.'

'Is that it?'

'That's it.'

'I need to take further lessons to be able to deal with you.'

'Wow! Do something, leave acting and modeling for a few days, put on make-up, and get admitted to our college.'

'Is it possible that I attend only your class and am free after that?'

'I don't know about you, but I'm sure I'll be free of my job.'

'In that case, as soon as you're free, the work on the restaurant can begin. Tell me, what should the salary be so that you can join?'

'When I joined the college here, the college committee said they would pay exactly half the salary I got in my previous job. With a six-month probationary period, meaning they would observe whether I was able to teach. But still, I accepted the job. I did it out of love. Because this is a job I know I can do. If I could do that, then I would survive.'

'Therefore, however, but—you can't take up this job, can you?'

'The day I feel confident that I can do that job, I myself will send you my CV and apply for the job. Maybe you can then be a bit lenient in regard to selection. After all, I don't have the proper qualifications for it.'

'That means salary is not an issue.'

'No.'

'I'm visiting Shreya tomorrow. Samir and Rohini are coming too. Would have been nice if you had been there. We could all have spent a day together at some seashore.'

'Have a nice time. Tell me all about it.'

'Whenever I see the sea now or hear about it, I only remember you.'

'That's a lot for me. I'm going to sort my books today. All the magazines have piled up for a long time. I haven't filed my writing for a long time as well. I plan to do all that through the night today. I'll take a shower after that and go to sleep in the morning.'

'What about eating? Have you forgotten how to cook or what?'

'There's a lot of food piled up. It might last for another month.'

'I spoke to Anandi yesterday.'

'Really?'

'She asked me over.'

'When are you going?'

'I'm not going.'

'Why not?'

'I don't feel like it.'

'Oh.'

'She has a daughter.'

'Is that why you don't feel like going?'

'No. It's just like that.'

'If you change your mind, go.'

'Won't you go to Kolkata, Tinni?'

'I don't have any plans yet.'

'Will you come to Pune with me?'

'No.'

'Why not?'

'Just like that.'

'Did you talk to Leena?'

'Quite a few times. She came over last week. She stayed for about an hour.'

'But she didn't tell me anything…'

'It wasn't anything important. Maybe she didn't remember; she must have forgotten to tell you.'

'Maybe.'

'That real estate agent of yours came again.'

'Can you help me out a bit?'

'Tell me; let me hear it.'

'You can decide whether you can do it or not after I tell you.'

'Exactly.'

'Can you go down to Juhu once?'

'For what?'

'You'll be picked up. A flat is coming up; can you go and look at it?'

'Why do you want me to look at it?'

'Because I'm unable to go.'

'I know nothing about such things. Don't ask me. I won't be able to do the job. And you'll be unhappy about that. I'll feel bad about it too.'

'There's nothing you have to do. You love the sea. That's why.'

'I can't see any connection between your flat and my love for the sea as yet.'

'Will you go if you see the connection?'

'I can't tell you just now.'

'I think I bothered you. I'm sorry.'

'I don't know if you did, but I didn't feel comfortable about it.'

'You sort your books. I'll talk to you again later.'

'Okay, bye.'

'Bye.'

Chapter 15

Let's hear some music. Iffat Ara. I haven't heard her for a long time. There are so many songs I haven't heard in ages. If I started listening to them, I could spend a month doing that. How does so much dust accumulate even at this height? It's only dust that accumulates; everything else gets spent. I must call the pest control chap tomorrow itself. I had to discard several books the last time as well. What on earth am I to do with all the books piled up on the floor? What if Rohini came and saw her flat in this condition? But is it really in bad condition? It's not scattered around. Books have piled up, that's all. I must get some simple racks fitted along the sides of the window. If I go to S.O.A.S., I can't take all these books along. But I'll need the books a lot there. What will I do then? I'll have to take some, at least. What if I don't like it there? What if they don't like me? What's the most that can happen? I'll have to come back, that's all. I hope my leave of absence is approved. There are plenty of hitches that can come up since it's a government college. Of course, that's also why it was possible to get a job mid-session. I'm sure to get battered somewhere or the other. Achira, you haven't learnt anything even after getting battered so many times in life. It's too much. But what if I don't get a leave of absence? I've got to think about that. If I leave my job once again, there'll be the problem of supporting myself. I can't do that at any cost. Hey, is Dev's offer a serious one? Where did Dev spring from again? Books, reading and writing, teaching, and going to S.O.A.S. to teach or research are all things I can do. Nothing else is mine. I'm floating around in Jonathan Livingston Seagull's sky. I no longer remember the name of the person who gave me the book. Neither on terribly sad nights nor during moments of great happiness did I ever remember his face. I never thought I had a friend in him—someone who may be far away, but who's a friend? So his existence and non-existence are the same. Age-old Bengal broke out in a smile through the *alpona* in the courtyard that morning. Was it right to go around searching after that? What Tinni's situation is today was built by aggregating hundreds upon hundreds of moments. Only the situation? No. Her spirit of life was also there. That was the first time I heard Hasan Raja's songs. I would never have understood the poem by Rabindranath unless I had heard the song. In the colors of my consciousness, an emerald couldn't have been as green.

'Hello!'

'What happened?'

'Aren't you sorting your books?'

'Yes, that's what I'm doing.'

'This is the fourth time I'm calling. Didn't you hear the phone?'

'No.'

'Did you leave your phone in another room?'

'No.'

'Were you meditating with your books?'

'Sort of.'

'How?'

'With every book I pick up, I remember so many things—stories, learnings, joys and sorrows. I'm sure you too have various kinds of memories of various kinds of work. Regarding costumes, scripts, posters, or music.'

'Maybe. I remember many forgotten things. One can laugh all by oneself. Cry too. Spend your time as you like. I'll call later; I mean tomorrow.'

'Thanks.'

'Bye.'

Chapter 16

Let me make some coffee. What do you say, Achira, like some coffee? Of course! So let's have a break. How beautifully Iffat Ara sings, isn't it Tinni? Achira, too, could have sung, if she tried. Yes, that's where the difference lies. She sings effortlessly. The song comes from deep within her, clad in melody. Without any special effort. That's why one can't help loving it. Effort is only good for completing one task after another. That's it; that's where it comes to an end. Did Achira spare any effort trying to be around Shubhro? It was by being around Shubhro that she wanted to bring to blossom the first kadam flower of the rainy season. But as Samir's Ma says, marriages are made in heaven. As if Shubhro's relation to me was only like an attempt at joining. It didn't join well; only the scar remained as something pure. Damn, again, that same old stench! Once the aroma of coffee spreads, there'll be no trace of that. Why two cups? One for Achira and one for Tinni. Mind it, Tinni is receiving undue attention. Dev is responsible for that. In the frame of twenty hours, he must have uttered "Tinni" at least two hundred times. What Dev did is his business. It's time for you to wind this up, Achira. If you can't make this journey alone, the entire *tapasya* will be false. What Ma'am said will turn out to be true. You're an extremely ordinary person. But for her, you'd be nothing. But why should any significance be given to what she said at all? She can say whatever she wants. She can convince my parents, too, that she is a God. And I have sinned by not heeding God. There's no redemption for me, ever. Who wants redemption? Why, Achira, it's you who's searching for release day and night. That's different. Everyone thinks that their thoughts pertaining to themselves are different—not like anyone else's. Seeking release arises from the stance of humble submission. I want to release myself from the feeling that anything I might do is based on thinking about someone else. Right from childhood, what my parents would like; then becoming "good" in the eyes of family members and relatives; thinking of people I knew before doing one thing and not doing another. As I grew up, somewhere along the way, under the weight of everyone's wishes and desires, I became shrunken. I didn't even realize it. I had no inkling that I was becoming something else, and when I became a mere instrument for the fulfilment of all of Ma'am's wishes by being around someone else, I thought love meant all of that. It was as if I couldn't believe that there were lots of things besides love that were required for running the household each day. That's why, when the belief snapped, suspicion became excessive. Achira, where's your balance? Don't you hear people say that balance is vital if you want to achieve something in life? Damn, I'm feeling sleepy now with all this muttering. I'll ask Raju to come one day. I can sort the books then. I can't do this all by myself. It's not just time that's required. It calls for the application of strength as well, to a large extent. I forgot about the coffee as well. Just as well. Or else I wouldn't have been able to sleep. Goodnight Tinni. Goodnight, sweet dreams. Hey, what's the matter? There's no matter. How would it be if that dream returned? Which dream? That I'm flying, just flying and flying, far, far away. My legs have turned as light as gossamer. There are no shackles. I'm flying around here and there like candy floss. After that. After that, I'm feeling sleepy—very, very sleepy.

'Yes, tell me.'

'Were you asleep?'

'No.

'But you sound as if you were fast asleep.'

'Not asleep, but deep in a dream.'

'Are dreams ever not deep?'

'They could be deeper.'

'But all that's for when you're awake.'

'No, not awake. One has to realize it in a state of meditation.'

'How much of the sea was there in the state of meditation?'

'It wasn't there. The sky was there. And I was floating around like a light feather.'

'Do you think you're any heavier than a feather?'

'Rubbish!'

'Even if I blow at you, you'll fly away.'

'That's why it's good to be afar.'

'But even if you fly away, I also know the mantra to snatch you from the air.'

'Such a mantra will bind me.'

'It won't bind you; it'll keep you awake. Hey, what's the news about your bougainvilleas?'

'I'll take a look and tell you.'

'Tell me later. Go to sleep. Are you in good health?'

'Absolutely.'

'I'm returning next week. We'll go together to see the Juhu flat.'

'You're returning next week? Why's that?'

'Part of the trip's canceled, that's why. I had nothing to do with that; it's the agency's business. But they'll pay me in full.'

'Great fun! You don't have to do any work; just receive your fee!'

'Why? Teachers also get their salaries during the vacations. And there's paid leave as well.'

'Are you comparing teachers to yourself?'

'No comparison. I was only searching for logic. How far did you get with sorting your books?'

'Not even a bit.'

'Why's that?'

'I got sleepy muttering to myself. So, I fell asleep.'

'I didn't know about this soporific effect of muttering.'

'Try it and see.'

'Of course I'll try it. But don't you have college today?'

'No.'

'How's that?'

'There's some festival holiday. Can't remember the name.'

'You're not telling the truth. You're not well. Are you hiding that from me?'

'Shall I really tell you?'

'Yes, tell me. I'm getting worried. Tell me quickly.'

'There's nothing to worry about. A bit of fever. So, I think I'll not go today.'

'What do you mean "you think"? You mustn't go. I'm going to ask Leena to go over to your place.'

'No. Please don't do any of that. Don't bother anyone the slightest bit on my account. I'll stay in bed, and I'll be fine.'

'There's nothing I can do from here.'

'I've felt unwell like this even when you were here. I didn't step out of my room for two days. You didn't know about it, didn't even realize anything.'

'And so, you won't let me do anything today either out of pique?'

'Why should I be piqued? I've stopped expecting anything from anyone. But when it comes to Rohini, she's different from everyone else.'

'I know Rohini, and I are not the same. But do you know that everyone on earth is not like your Ma'am and Shubhro?'

'No, I don't, because I don't want to know about that.'

'So you only like to subject yourself to pain?'

'Even if I do, that's my wish. Not because someone else likes it or doesn't like it.'

'Please, Tinni, don't be stubborn. I'm going to call my physician. He'll go to your place and take a look at you. Please let me do something. Not because I'll be happy. Because you are all alone, you need that. Allow me to do just this much, at least as a neighbor.'

'Are you my next door neighbor?'

'I don't know. Be quiet and stay in bed. The doctor will be there very soon.'

'Thanks.'

'I'll talk to you again very soon.'

Chapter 17

Why are all men strange in different ways? One was so indifferent that even though someone was beside him day after day, she had to pinch him to see if he was alive. And another worries about me so much that it makes me uncomfortable. Maybe that is part of nature on this earth. There too, it's three parts water and one part land. There's no balance whatsoever. Water, and that, too, is mostly brackish, which is not really useful. My body, too, couldn't find a better time to fall ill. I hate this business of doctors and such. Who knows what problems a celebrity doctor might create? Let it be. Who knows how much longer she's going to experiment with herself? Will I play spectator again? No, I can't do that anymore. Will the doctor come by helicopter and land here? I would have gotten better if I could sleep properly. All this overreaction...

'Yes, tell me.'

'What was your temperature?'

'I don't know. I didn't ask the doctor.'

'Why not?'

'The doctor's given the medicines.'

'Did you take them?'

'I will. Don't worry so much. I'll feel really bad then.'

'Is everything about me so bad that you only feel bad?'

'No. You want to do so much that I really don't know what my reaction ought to be. I get really scared. Maybe the fear that I might make another mistake itself makes me make many mistakes.'

'You're mad.'

'You're right. I'm mad.'

'Many people would have survived if they could have been mad like you. We realize too late. Rohini is the only one who can easily fathom it, like a lapidary.'

'Rohini's completely different from the world that I know. Like a blessing from God. Like the light of the sun. One doesn't even have to ask. It arrives on its own.'

'Your words too seem to show me a direction.'

'Me? Whose own direction is awry?'

'But I feel it. Believe me, I'm not flirting. I'm very serious.'

'My fever may turn serious. Shouldn't we stop here for now?'

'If your fever goes up or you need anything else, please call me or Suraj. I'll do whatever I can from here itself.'

'And if you're here?'

'If I were there, I would have applied cool washcloths to your forehead. Once the temperature came down, I would sit by your feet so that you'd see me as soon as you woke up.'

'Neither am I Krishna nor are you Arjuna!'

'Still, I would have liked to keep watch over you.'

'I'm feeling very sleepy.'

'Go to sleep. Some soup will be delivered to you.'

'By whom?'

'You don't have to worry about that. Get up and have it.'

'Someone didn't know anything even while we were in the

same room, and here you are nursing me while overseas. Perhaps this is how life returns everything deposited in it in the same lifetime itself.'

'Like the sea?'

'The sea turns me into a pauper and gives me whatever is mine.'

'It would have been good if I were your sea.'

'All my words and work would have been abortive.'

'I say meaningless things. Go to sleep.'

'I have to go to sleep knowing I have to wake up again.'

'Wake up bit by bit.'

'Bye, thanks for everything.'

'Bye.'

Chapter 18

Fever and blabbering for quite a few days. I think there was a phone call from college. I couldn't submit the exam papers on time. Question papers have to be sent as well. And then there's the moderation, scrutiny, and finally, the results—once again the same old game of numbers. I have to send an email to S.O.A.S. But I need to get the leave approval before that. Dev will be returning. If only I could have completed everything before that. Is it because Dev did me a good turn that I'm so suspicious of him? Let's assume that Jupiter is now ruling over my life. That's why I'm getting more than I'm due. But I never sought such extravagance. So, am I beginning to rot from within? I didn't realize it. But what's my fault? And what qualities do I have at all, for that matter? I can't take it anymore. Talk, talk, and talk. The secret of the bougainvillea is still quite far away from the balcony. That's best. The ardent breeze that returns after paying homage at the Haji Ali dargah nudges my anchal; it is in my feathers and wings. These nights would have been great if one could have spent them writing away. The night that fills my breath. What more do I want anyone to hear? No. I'm the listener. The teller as well. I'll go directly to Chowpatty tomorrow after college. No, Marine Drive. I'll gaze at the rocks and listen to the sea. Be well. Be well, free time. Be well, sad eyes. Let me wear my spectacles; I can't sleep now.

'Hello!'

'What's the matter? Do you think it's possible that if you don't answer the phone, I'll cease to exist?'

'It's only the impossible that I encounter, again and again.'

'In that case, perhaps I'm the biggest example of that.'

'Therefore, my efforts are futile.'

'I'm not demanding that as soon as I open the door, I want you, yet…'

'Do you remember we laughed when you made fun of all my yets, buts and therefores?

'It's inevitable.'

'What? Therefore, yet, but, etcetera?'

'This evening, the sea in Juhu has invited you and asked me to come along.'

'But I have a lot of work.'

'What if I lend a hand with that?'

'It can't be done.'

'Why not?'

'Think of the poor students. Either all of them will fail, or else all of them will get double the maximum marks.'

'Oh! Checking exam papers?'

'Yes. Exam papers.'

'Take a look at the sea, and then do it.'

'It'll be dangerous if I end up getting depressed.'

'Why should you get depressed?'

'I might, you never know.'

'I'll heal you.'

'Your audacity!'

'What about it?'

'It's intolerable.'

'Then I'll buy some tolerance ointment.'

'If I see the sun setting at Juhu, I'll feel like getting into the sea.'

'Then do that.'

'And I might not feel like returning.'

'I'll lift you up from the red water like soft foam.'

'And after that?'

'After that rippling water.'

'When are you returning?'

'Whenever you ask me to.'

'You have a right to this house. Why do you have to wait for me to tell you?'

'Still, unless you ask me to, I won't return.'

'Meaning?'

'Meaning, I have been standing outside the door and talking all this while.'

'That can't be.'

'The watchman saw me four times. You can ask him.'

'But you have your keys with you'.

'I lost all my keys.'

'Oh! Say that. Wait a minute.'

'Isn't that a lot of time for any kind of explosion?'

'You're a cinema man. Nothing but gunfire, murder, and mayhem.'

'There's a romantic sequence this very evening; you'll see the proof instantly.'

'Proof's of no use.'

'I feel like mischief.'

'Your directors benefit a lot by working with you, don't they?

'Why all these film-related references, all of a sudden!'

'You save them the expense of having dialogues written.'

'That's the producer's gain.'

'But you improvise according to the situation…'

'In this situation, talk is inappropriate.'

'I'm going for a shower.'

'Let me hear the sound.'

'When will you leave?'

'Whatever's correct for you.'

'But everything's incorrect; everything's un-wrong.'

'In that case, what's the point of delaying anymore? I'm waiting in the car.'

'But it'll take me some time.'

'For your makeup, you mean?'

'I wear that all the time. You don't realize it.'

'Did the weather office forecast a storm over the Arabian Sea?'

'Once the storm is over there's only peace.'

'Wear something very blue.'

'You don't have plans to cast me into the sea, do you?'

'Then that would mean fulfilment of my *sadhana*.'

'How?'

'I'm the one who'll cast you into the sea, and it's to me that you'll return.'

'I'll come walking for now. You go.'

'More waiting?'

'No.'

'Has the century of seeing you as soon as I open my eyes arrived or what?'

'Keep your eyes closed then.'

'Ready?'

'Almost.'

'Even now?'

'Till the end. How many other people will there be in the flat?'

'You and me for now.'

'Don't talk rubbish. Who else is going to be there in the flat that you're taking me to?'

'No one. Suraj might come.'

'How much of the sea is visible from there?'

'All of it. Meaning, every window in every room is curtained by the sea.'

'Wow!'

'Choose the room you'd like to stay in first. The remaining ones will be allotted after that.'

'Why would I want to stay there? And what do you mean by allotted?'

'I mean, which one will be mine, which one the guestroom, living room, study—all that.'

'A fine plan! But not for me.'

'In that case, the plan regarding the flat is canceled.'

'If you say that, I'll feel like a criminal.'

'Do you want to see the flat first or go to the beach first?'

'Better to see the flat first.'

'From the micro to the macro; after all, we are Indian.'

'We are what we are. Wherever that might be. Why are you quiet?'

'I'm worried.'

'Why?'

'What if you don't like it?

'If I don't like what?'

'The excessive view of the sea.'

'Redo the interior.'

'We're there. Now close your eyes.'

'Here. Completely shut.'

'Look. Far away, more far away.'

'I have to go.'

'Where?'

'To S.O.A.S.'
'For how long?'
'I don't know.'
'Is that why you agreed so readily to come here?'
'No. It's your flat. As a neighbor, I too have some responsibility.'
'Don't be so unkind. It doesn't suit you.'
'I couldn't figure out what suits me.'
'I know.'
'How did you know?'
'Through meditation.'
'What did you realize?'
'A whole sea.'
'Very salty!'
'Like my tears.'

Dr. Swati Guha is currently the Director, Institute of Language Studies and Research (ILSR), Kolkata, West Bengal which is a research institute under the Department of Higher Education, Government of West Bengal. Dr. Guha has a vast range of academic and administrative expertise and has previously been Director, Nazrul Centre for Social and Cultural Studies, Kazi Nazrul University, Asansol, West Bengal and Development Officer, Sidho Kanho Birsha University, West Bengal. She has also served the Roopkala Kendro, an institute of social communication, under the Department of Information & Cultural Affairs, Government of West Bengal. In addition to her administrative roles, Dr. Guha is also well known as a creative writer and has written many fictional and non-fictional books and has earned recognition through various literary and cultural awards. Being an alumnus of Presidency College and Jadavpur University, Dr. Guha has avid academic interest and through her own research and academic as well as creative writings, Dr. Guha evinces comprehensive involvement in academic writing and research deliberations.

V. Ramaswamy took up literary translation of voices from the margins after two decades of grassroots and public activism in support of the labouring poor in his city, Kolkata. He has translated Subimal Misra's The *Golden Gandhi Statue from America: Early Stories*, *Wild Animals Prohibited: Stories, Anti-Stories*, and *This Could Have Become Ramayan Chamar's Tale: Two Anti-Novels*, and Manoranjan Byapari's novels, *The Runaway Boy*, and *The Nemesis*. His translation of Adhir Biswas's *Memories of Arrival: A Voice from the Margins*, was published in 2022, as were Shahidul Zahir's *Life and Political Reality: Two Novellas* (co-translated with Shahroza Nahrin), and *Why There Are No Noyontara Flowers in Agargaon Colony: Stories*. The novel *I See the Face*, also by Zahir, was published in 2023. Ramaswamy has attended residencies at Sangam House, India, Writers Omi, USA, and Toji Cultural Foundation, Korea. He was selected for the Toji Fellowship in Wonju, Korea, in 2015, and the Literature Across Frontiers – Charles Wallace India Trust fellowship in creative writing & translation at Aberystwyth University, Wales, in 2016. Ramaswamy received the translation fellowship of the New India Foundation, and the PEN Presents translation grant in 2022. Life and Political Reality: Two Novellas was awarded the prize for best translated book for 2022 by the Bangla Translation Foundation (Dhaka).